OFF THE MAT

OFF THE MAT

Jeff Bibbey

Thanks to the editors: The Penpointers – the greatest group of guys ever to set cynicism aside and trust their hearts, Judith K, Mom, Lisa K.

Thanks to the coaches: Mark C, Tom L, Ken T, Marc L, Cindy G

Thanks to my wife Kristy and our kids for the patience, encouragement, and living the life with me.

For the boys. Every one of you.

I

1

February, 2008

"I'm a runner for Christ now. That's what I do; I run for Christ. It's tattooed on my leg, see here. Runner 4 and His picture. Twenty-two miles yesterday. Today just six. But before I left I wrestled for about an hour, training with the team." Devin Thomsen glanced up at the vaulted ceiling of Union Station, then back down to his calf. "Coach, Steven was really good, you know?"

"I know." The coach, Sean Cardsen, tried to say more, but his voice cracked and caught. He was speechless, like those before angels. The vision made all the more luminous by contrast with the cavern around them. The place had been renovated but on this night it was lipstick on a crone. A few heels clicked on the tile, incoherent echoes the only voices. Squeaking wet tennis shoes and dragging plastic bags harmonized as the homeless and near-homeless shuffled by, gathering warmth for their next venture outside. Amtrak brought no romance to the old station, and tonight only the buses came, bringing a few on the personal business of subsistence. There were no vacations going on.

The Runner for Christ stood before Cardsen in a green warm-up jacket that said "Medford" open to show a grey T-shirt that said "Northwest Freestyle." The sleeves hung beyond Devin's wrists, and his elbows bowed out the way they will on the spare creatures found in the sport of wrestling. His faded Levis were too large, easy to pull up and show the tattoo. Feet dark with grime allowed occasional skin to show through sandal straps. His hair was white-blonde and cut short, his skin white as well, almost transparent, taut over his skull and blue neck

3

veins. Iridescent in the light of the station, he oozed an intensity that increased his presence.

Cardsen waited hours for this moment. They hugged and smiled together as Devin debarked the bus. The coach expected to do most of the talking but now even the small talk of a simple welcome evaporated. He became lost in thoughts of Devin sleeping on filthy floors, of meth and recovery meetings before the boy learned to drive. The Runner looked at him for a moment with a curious smirk, waiting to be led into conversation. Cardsen's eyes glazed over, and he stayed quiet.

The Runner let his pant leg fall back over his tattoo and took his travel bag from the floor to his shoulder, taking the initiative to speak. "Do they remember me? Does anyone?"

"They do, and will even more when they see you. It takes a lot of sacrifice for you to come all the way up here. I'm amazed that you did it, and for this. For Alan Matchik, for Steven."

"Especially for this, Coach, especially for this."

Outside Union Station the pavement gleamed wet in the streetlights, drizzle obscuring the buildings across the street. The coach led the way to a GMC pickup, eighteen years old and still in solid shape. Cardsen bought it used twelve years before from a meticulous old man and did his best to be opposite, but his abuse glanced off, and the truck looked clean and traditional in the rain. Cardsen's key went in the door, his jaw working back and forth seeking more to say, but nothing came. The events of the past years were a weight. The atmosphere hanging over them suffocated them, how could it not? But this young man, the very idea of him, lifted Cardsen. The old fight, that senseless tenacity, glimmered inside him again. He invited a brighter glow and the return of actual passion. Devin's arrival cemented a miraculous alliance, fuel to drive him forward.

Devin looked out the side window of the truck, his breath condensing on the glass as they crossed over the bridge below them. Everything outside the truck became invisible. "His brother Alan? What's he like now?"

"Wish I knew more, but he's got to be good or he wouldn't be where he is today. I'm not sure if we will even speak to him. So much has gone on you know."

"Yeah, I know."

Thirty minutes later the freeways gave way to the suburban roads and then ten minutes later to the edge of Braxton Township. Subdivisions encroached on all sides, choking Cardsen's place like the blackberry bushes used to. His bi-level house had been intended as a step up for the owners of a dairy in 1978 but the dairy was gone now and a park covered where the main barn had been. In those times, eighteen hundred square feet meant you had it made. Success now meant one of the five thousand square foot houses covering the historical fields of the dairy farm.

They went into the house with quiet voices, the effect canceled as they shed gear on the small landing. Steps led up to the family room, graced by twisted wrought iron rails. Wet coats steamed and dripped as they hung them on the pegs. The coach tossed Devin's bag to the top of the steps with a thump.

Sonia came out in sweats to meet them as they came up to living room level.

"Sonia, this is Devin. You might remember, from a few years back?"

"Hi, Devin. I…" She stopped herself from 'have heard a lot about you,' and went with "Yes, I remember. You've grown up!" She shook his hand and then offered him food and drink, which he declined.

By this time Tanya and Cory had come out of their bedrooms and stared at them from the hall. Cardsen made introductions and Devin disarmed the kids with a smile.

"You guys are so big now!" The Runner went to Cory and bent over with his hands on his knees. "I remember when you were tiny. You would run out on the mat once in a while and all the action would have to stop!"

"I know," said a confident eight-year-old Cory. "I used to say 'Momma, why do big boys wrestle?'"

Devin laughed and pointed at him. "She couldn't answer you, could she?"

***

The Runner looked at his face in the mirror. He pulled the skin of his cheeks tight on each side, satisfied that no blemishes had risen unannounced. He met his own eyes, just for a moment. Contact with his own eyes is how it often began. He turned on the water, took some in his shaking hands, and splashed it up on his face. The reflection showed the burn scars all over the back of his hands, dropping the bottom out of his stomach. Surely Coach noticed them. As he moved into the hall he saw a computer station in the next room. The dim hall light revealed pictures on the wall. He paused, listened for sounds from upstairs, and satisfied there were none, turned on the light and went in. Next to the dusty teaching awards, he saw a curled photo taped to the wall. It was their team. He reached out and touched it. He saw himself in the front sitting Indian-style. Little, a ninety-pounder. He saw the long blonde hair, out of style then, and in style now, but he was opposite again. The picture was too small to see his eyes. Third from the left, in the front row, sat Steven. Alan was also easy to find. His stomach lurched and his jaw muscles tightened.

Seeing the picture started it. A quiet moaning pain rose slowly like from a deep well. There was no cap on that pit, and what was down there was coming up sure as the world, disembodied, raging. Climbing up out of the depths, heading for a scream, his unwanted guest began to pound on him from the inside. Devin thought about the Israelites who put blood on the door so that the destroying angel would fly over. The Runner for Christ had tried that; digging into himself for blood to offer. He ran his fingers over the scars on his forearms, remembering. That disembodied thing from his gut smelled the blood, circled around waiting for it to dry, and came on harder.

He dropped into a sitting position on the futon mattress on the floor and dug in his bag for the little New Testament; his antacid. The print was too small and he couldn't focus. Scripture reading only worked for him if he read it aloud, and he couldn't do that here. The people upstairs might be curious, and he'd rather not face them like this. Definitely not Coach.

The worst of it loomed ahead, soon, but some wisdom reminded him that he'd weathered it before. What was he going to do anyway? Head out the door and walk two miles to Braxton Town Center and see if tweakers still gathered under the bridge? Show up like a ghost asking to score and have Coach call out the troops for a manhunt? Or worse, have Coach sit at home and give up altogether on all the kids that had wrung him out?

Devin slipped his jeans off. He threw himself to the floor, to push-up position. Without loud breathing or grunting, he went to work.

He did dozens. Hundreds. One hand. Feet up on a chair. Marine style. Spider style. Narrow hands. Wide hands. He stopped for thirty seconds or so when he felt dizzy, panted quietly, and saw visions of his matches at the state tournament. The sweet pain endured when the knee popped again. The comeback in the quarterfinals, the doubles and high crotch takedowns he hit; his mom's hair visible in the stands, the coaches screaming to finish off that guy from Molalla who hadn't been beaten all year. Unbeaten, but Devin near-cradled him just like he would some sophomore at a camp. In the semifinals when he ran into the Krazen kid, the high school legend from Roseburg, the dream slipped away. The Runner had been filled with the belief that he just needed to out-hustle his opponent like he always did. Krazen gave him a brutal lesson, proving to him that hustle wouldn't be enough. Too much knowledge and experience missed. For years, Krazen built skill, footwork and muscle memory. Krazen hadn't been smoking crank, doing the twelve steps, or rebuilding a body from scratch. The beginnings of these and other images of himself were aborted and guided back to wrestling by physical and mental ritual. All these things all this conflict, would run by in thirty seconds, and he would call out quietly to Jesus. Thank you, Jesus, and he would push and push some more. And Christ was always dying on the cross through the whole thing, perpetual death, perpetual ecstasy, perpetually purposeful and weirdly joyful.

After an hour, nothing more attacked him from inside. A wave of exhaustion took him. Devin found himself in front of the bathroom mirror drying the beads of sweat that covered his face and arms with a small towel. He rubbed his glistening hair, then gulped water until he thought he'd burst. He took the sweaty towel with him and put it under his bag so that no one else in the house would have to use it, and collapsed on the futon.

***

Upstairs, the coach lay back with his hands behind his head, listening to the gentle drum of the rain. He still noticed after all of these years and appreciated the rain for how it helped him sleep. The sound remained a secret reason why he never moved his family away.

Sonia moved her hand gently on his chest. "What a good-looking young man, and so grown up, but he looks and moves like a cat. He's got that blonde hair, and his cheekbones are all chiseled and a nice smile."

"Yeah, he carries no fat on him. I mean none. He runs compulsively. For Christ, that is. He's always been a good-looking kid, but just a little guy when we met. Now I'd say he might wrestle in the one-forties."

"One-forties?" Sonia blew air through her lips. "That's smaller than I am or ever will be again! How can they be built like that and weigh less than me? I can't remember all of what you've told me about Devin, it's been too much to keep track of. Those eyes of his, wow, they catch you. And they've seen some things, haven't they?"

Cardsen sighed. "He's in college now, after all he's been through. So hard to believe, such an incredible thing. I'd like to show him off to some people. That's where Steven should be right now." He gulped. He needed to stop talking.

She continued stroking his chest, and spoke to him softly. "What you guys did together then, that was good work. You have to know that. Some of those kids had so little in their lives. What if they never even had those seasons with you?"

2

October, 2002

The wide steps to the band room were home to gangly arms and legs splayed all over. Half-spilled school backpacks and skateboards for the ride home lay all about. Three pairs of eighth grade veterans wrestled on the steps in their school clothes. In one case, the boy getting the worst of it had his head pointed down the stairs while his backbone painfully spanned three higher steps. Others talked or laughed or stared off in silence, some standing, some sitting. The pack of seventh graders brave enough to come out for wrestling sat near the lower right huddled around a pillar. The pillar offered scant protection against an impatient veteran wrestler grabbing them to deliver a foretaste of what lay ahead. As the minutes ticked off tension built from excitement and fear. A few candidates stood and moved about for relief.

Cardsen walked around the corner, followed by his assistant coach, Matt Waters. Immediately, the older boys did what they could to slow the chaos, audible murmurs, "It's coach." "Hey stop, it's coach." "Sit down, if you know what's good for you."

Cardsen's voice boomed. "Get it quiet."

The coach towered over the knot of seventh graders and he gestured with the clipboard to gather the boys in tight. He saw all those that had wrestled the year before. Cardsen rolled their names over in his mind, no one was missing, a feat, considering the unreliability of a few of them.

The coach couldn't help but register the presence of Steven Matchik, along with his younger brother Alan. Steven leaned back, elbows on the step behind him. His black hair and tan skin stood out against a yellow polo shirt. His brown eyes were set in a serious expression, making him look like he was searching for answers. Cardsen knew Steven rarely smiled, and on those occasions he always attracted attention. Steven fell two inches below average in height for his age, but perfectly proportioned. The small strain from the position in which he sat caused veins to emerge from his neck and biceps, like they had been looking for the smallest excuse. The roundness of the back of his hamstrings showed through his corduroy pants. Always remarkably strong and quick, he caught the eyes of his PE teachers from early in elementary school. As a defensive back on the Braxton football team, he hit and hustled for Cardsen like no other. An indifference to the skills required for basketball and baseball led him to wrestling, and he won the district championship in his first year competing. Now he looked at Cardsen intensely and carried the close-lipped smile of someone who knew what was coming.

Cardsen made eye contact, clear on what Steven must be thinking. *Here it is. I can win it again. Coach will push me, and I'll never let up. Not once, not ever.*

At the top of the steps, Austin Reichs, their misplaced cowboy, leaned against a door, arms folded, scowling down at Cardsen's feet, eyes out of view. There was always at least one like Austin Reichs. Cardsen didn't need speech to hear him.

A good teacher could hear, "I'm here to kick ass. I'm not here to listen to you. I wrestle for me, not this team." A better teacher would also hear, "I need this because I've got nothing. I need a coach, because I've got no one I can count on." Cardsen heard that, too.

Cardsen handed the sign-up sheet around, inquired about physical exams and paperwork, and paused to verbally hammer the two veterans who hadn't done that properly. He talked about shoes, clothes, weight policies, academic eligibility, and the mats. Cardsen spoke concisely and efficiently. It was his ninth year delivering the opening meeting.

A seventh grader named Eric Lofton raised his hand. He looked about eighty pounds wet, and had wisps of sandy hair that fell all over his tan face. "I've got violin lessons at four on Mondays. So, um, what do you think will happen if I don't change them?"

The predictable snickering and eye rolling began. The older guys smelled blood in the water. This kid was going to be skewered.

Cardsen stared at him. "Are you any good?"

Lofton stammered and looked down. "Not really, I mean, I guess. Well, I'm first chair in Beginning Orchestra, and um you know, I can play part of Hoe Down."

"Lofton, look at me."

Lofton looked up with the saddest brown eyes.

"I expect you to keep getting better on that thing. And after all this is over, you and I are going to jam Hoe Down before the district tournament is that clear?"

Cardsen saw predatory smiles morph to reflect the thrill at his unpredictability. A few laughs came. Also whispers, "Is he serious?"

"We'll do it gentlemen. Count on it."

Lofton's eyes widened.

"That would be cool. But don't tell anybody I listened to no Hoe Down," said Alfred Rice, the team's laconic heavyweight, and sole African-American. The team laughed.

Matt Waters once mused aloud to Cardsen that the sheltered suburban skaters and white trash that blew in and out of Braxton to live with their mom's ex-boyfriend's mom's friend's daughter, wouldn't know a black person from Adam. Rice could be half Bengali and half Samoan for all they knew.

"Gentlemen, the point is, there are a lot of outside things you guys are committed to. I don't expect you to give them up. I want you to stick with them. But that doesn't mean you get to sacrifice your work here. So, try hard to change the time. If that doesn't work, stay as late as you possibly can before taking off. Obviously, for meets, we have to have you. Most important of all communicate to me what's going on, I don't like surprises."

Now came time for the brief motivational section. Cardsen didn't need to fake anything here. He firmly believed everything he had to say. He spoke his lines emphatically, not so much because he liked the sound of his own voice, although he'd been accused of that, but because he knew the changes that would happen to all of them in the next ten weeks.

"You start something special today. That you're here demonstrates courage already. You will begin to become something new, and people outside of here won't really understand it. Many of your parents won't understand. You will have to help them, educate them. Your friends outside here won't understand. They will say things about the uniforms, or being so close to other guys or whatever, but it's ignorance. People fear what they can't understand. This is the world's oldest sport. It is a martial art. It is the martial art of the cradle of civilization. Greece. Turkey. Israel. Iran. Remember that." Cardsen's arms moved in sweeping gestures and intimidating points. He could have been preaching a tent revival or hawking a topless show off old Burnside Street in downtown Portland.

"You will push yourself harder than you ever have before, I don't care what sports you've done. I don't care if you've played football, even if you played football for me. We'll go way farther. You'll look inside and find something you didn't even know was there. Old guys, am I lying to you?"

The veterans smiled and nodded at the descriptions and several responded. "No, it's true, it's true."

Lofton thrust his hand up. "I once took rappelling and rock climbing, extreme like, at Yosemite Ranger School. Do you think it will be harder than that?"

"Coach Waters, write this down, Eric Lofton has a Question Restriction Asterisk. He gets two per practice, maximum." Cardsen turned back to Lofton. "I think it will be slightly tougher than the one at Yosemite but just a little less than the Authentic Mining School at Black Hills National Monument."

Matt Waters, grinning, made a show of noting on his clipboard.

Lofton, and most of the others, just looked perplexed. Steven Matchik broke a bit of a smile, and so did Ryan Van Gorder, the representative intellect and conscience of the Braxton wrestling team.

"Gentlemen, you will find out that this team will get close. We will look out for each other. Older guys will help the young guys learn. There will be no crap pulled on anybody in the locker room or you will answer to me. I am not forcing friendships or asking people to hang out together that normally don't. But when you see each other in the halls you will defend and honor each other. I don't care if you are too fat, too weak, tougher than anybody, or know a lot of wrestling. You will play a role. If you are district champion, or just struggling to get wins on JV, you'll get coaching from us and I intend to prove it to you. I am most interested in how you improve and provide effort from beginning to end. I know that with this crew, if we just do the right things, the wins will come. Because actually," Cardsen looked around slowly, "this is a pretty damn good crew already."

There was an electric response.

"Yeah." "We win it this year." "No one touches us this year." High fives. Austin Reichs rolled his eyes, but then responded to the offer by Ryan Van Gorder of a hand to slap.

"Go get your gear on. Leave your other stuff right here. You'll get lockers after practice. We got time for a short one."

The boys scrambled, falling all over each other to get off the steps.

With the team gone, Waters started laughing. "Niiiice."

"What can I say? Gotta know how to hold a crowd."

By now the men were walking toward the locker room and coach's office in order to dress out for practice. They turned a corner and blocking the way was Evelyn Cummings, BJH's finest counselor, with a long-haired blonde boy, eyes downcast, hands thrust into dirty, faded jeans. Cardsen knew the instant he saw the boy that he had wrestler written all over him. Cardsen had an interesting gift, knowing at a glance whether an adolescent, and sometimes a prepubescent, had high odds of wanting to be part of the sport. Something in the body build, the carelessness with hair and clothes, the way they stood. But those things didn't always match, and still he could tell. Also with the counselor was a woman he suspected to be the boy's mother. She had wrinkles and tough skin, blonde hair curled back in a modified Farrah Fawcett, jeans and an old Styx T-shirt. A bit tight for a school. She smiled and revealed a forgotten beauty. Evelyn took the mother by the elbow and turned her to face the coaches.

"Sean, this is Alexa Thomsen, and this is Devin. He's new and he says he wants to wrestle."

As Cardsen shook Ms. Thomsen's hand Devin glanced up but didn't make full eye contact. Cardsen saw piercing blue eyes flash so bright he thought it might hurt if someone looked at them.

"He'll be in your second period Physical Science."

Evelyn winked at him. She knew that Cardsen would want the kid in his class. Not only did he want his wrestlers in his class when possible, but he liked getting tough kids of either gender if he thought they could connect. Of course, if it didn't work out, it was just as miserable for Cardsen as any other teacher, but he never ducked such a challenge. The counselors often knew what would make a good match for either Cardsen or his counterpart, Liselle Wilkins.

Cardsen knew what he had to do. Honor mom but immediately make contact with the kid without going through mom. He knew that any growth and connection through the sport would have to come from the young man stepping up alone.

"You've wrestled before?"

Cardsen noticed the struggle the kid went through just to look up and the inordinate amount of time for a response. Complications, thought Cardsen. For some reason the kid needs to think on this simple question. For the first time Cardsen locked into those eyes.

"I wrestled last year at my other school. I was our eighty pounder for a while. And I did a little bit of club in elementary. I think I'm more like ninety now."

"That's outstanding. Perfect. We have a close team here and we have all types of kids. We work very hard but we also have fun. I'm Coach Cardsen and this is Coach Waters."

Then Cardsen shook his hand; shook his smaller hand like an adult.

Leaving Devin behind with the counselor, Matt Waters led the way to the coach's office with Sean Cardsen close behind. As the wrestling coaches entered, they saw Shockley, the rookie PE teacher, packing a gym bag near the other end of the room. The young teacher looked up and then back down without acknowledging them.

"Sean, looks like you've been recruiting. We had a pretty solid looking bunch out there on the steps."

"Yeah, how 'bout it, Matt? Some characters and some tough stuff. Sheeit, I got a feeling, man. We could be pretty good. We just might have something."

Sean Cardsen sat down heavily on Shockley's chair, pulled off his shoes, and propped his stocking feet up on the PE teacher's desk. His hands interlocked behind his head, pushing up his straight and unruly brown hair. The coach was bulky and thick, with a broad back and arms that looked like they could still do some damage. Not exactly an impressive specimen like a body builder, or the other way, like a runner, but at thirty-seven he hadn't completely gone to seed either. Yet he was a science teacher, and no one would mistake him for a working man living a hard life. A surgery scar ran like a snake around his left elbow. His Adam's apple stood out excessively, and his lips stayed together and moved in and out a bit constantly chewing on what to say next.

Thank God for Matt, thought Cardsen as he looked over at his assistant who had begun to change out of his teaching clothes. *Life would be pretty tough without him.* Matt Waters taught a program to introduce kids to vocational education, a mixture of shop, life-skills, and career studies, and had been a terrific addition when he transferred in two years ago.

"You know, I hit them up pretty hard at the end of football. Same story every year. I bust their butt out there, so when I ask who wants to spend ten more weeks with me everybody kind of looks at the ground. But the ones that count are here."

Who cares? Cardsen thought. A small corner of the world. A small sport with a small season. Not like high school, where the kids remember their teachers and mentors, telling stories about them all their lives. No, the place everyone thinks they hated and don't remember, middle school, junior high. If it was so awful like a lot say, why did he see so much joy everyday; all the energy, learning, activity, and emotional intensity. For

17

example, take his classroom, with its Bunsen burner outlets, linoleum floors, rock and roll memorabilia and mineral crystals. Hot, smelly and hated in August, but those that found a home cried in June when they left. Braxton, his place, it was a good place.

But wrestling is a small sport. And he a small coach. In fact, he was just barely a winning coach if you looked at the records. When coaching high school football a few years back, the veteran coach he worked with told Cardsen that he was the best young football coach he'd seen, and that sticking with it could mean a lot of attention. But this sport, this office, his classroom, those are what ended the ambition for coaching higher. He couldn't leave these small things. *I care, so does Matt. The boys care, even if only their subconscious will remember. One day I'll be fifty-seven, and I'll close that door over there for the last time. I'll ask myself –did I do enough?*

Shockley came over to his desk, now fouled with Cardsen's feet, to retrieve something. Cardsen observed how the small, uptight rookie began to blow more air in and out of his nose as he noticed that his meticulously arranged pencil cup and lesson book had been moved. Cardsen sat perfectly still as the rookie leaned over him and retrieved a cell phone from a shelf. Sensing Matt watching from the lockers, Cardsen couldn't resist the entertainment value.

"What's up?" Cardsen shot off, appearing disinterested.

"Uh, well, just had to get this phone." The poor rookie retained enough pride to have red blotches of anger rising on his face.

Cardsen carried himself like he owned the place, and people sometimes talked in ways that confirmed it. He knew this kid wouldn't challenge him. Shockley moved away toward the door, clearly eager to escape another day in hell.

"Later." said Cardsen.

Then, right there with his feet up, he ripped a loud one that sounded like a roadie testing the distortion pedal before the big show.

Matt Waters couldn't hold it anymore and he laughed aloud, an attempt at suppression changed it to a crying sound just as the door closed. "That...was the most unprofessional thing I've seen."

Cardsen turned to Matt, very pleased with himself. "You're gagging; you sound like a chimp being strangled. Let it go, man, let it out."

The assistant coach snorted and shook his head with a toothy smile.

"You're pretty new around here too, Matt, so keep watching. You know, sometimes you can just tell. I lay 70-30 odds that poor bastard doesn't make the end of the year. And I give it 90-10 that he's not back next year. And I called it 60-40 at the opening meeting just on his introduction. Ask Gordon, down the hall from me, if you need proof. Gees, we need someone steady in here."

"What do you think he'd rather do?"

"Got a rich daddy. Maybe he'll start him a rafting company on the Deschutes."

Matt laughed again. "Yeah, and in the off-season he'll be working those ski-lifts up on Hood."

Cardsen pulled his feet to the floor and moved to his locker to change clothes.

"Matt, did you see that new kid?"

"I saw him. He looks like he could really be something." Then Matt changed his optimistic tone to sound ironic. "In a lot of ways."

"Well, if you haven't been getting enough social work down at your end of the building wait until we tie in to this crew."

3

Devin watched the coaches head down the hall toward the locker room, and he felt a surge of eagerness to dress out and practice with them.

Already a year since I last wrestled, and so much has changed. I miss LaGrande, well, those kids there, the ones that used to like me. When I could go to birthday parties and even have one, the trampoline we used to have, a lawn and sprinklers. Legos, oh well, seem too old now. Dad's car parts all over. Dad? I'm shaking, I can't do that or this coach'll think I'm a wimp. How tough are the kids here? I remember when I broke Ronny Nolasco's nose last year, he bled, and it was all over me and I liked it. But he was really weak. Then I felt bad. Because he was one of my last friends that would come over or invite me, and that was kind of it for that. Because he knew I did it on purpose, when I didn't have to. I pinned most of my guys, but our coach was so easy and unorganized. And then I missed the last four matches. Gone three weeks to Grandma's, then ineligible. Damn, everyone seems huge here, and I'm small. And this coach is going to be my teacher for science. What if he's mean? Well, I guess I've seen mean before.

It's like he already knows me, but how could that be? Because he doesn't know any of it. And it's like he wants me here. It's cool, but is that weird? Why does he want to know a kid?

4

Two weeks in and the first match is in three days.

The mats are down and Cardsen has the team circled up. The boys remain quiet as they do a light stretch series with their legs spread wide. Cardsen doesn't like them counting every stretch, too much noise. There will be plenty of hooah and yelling and counting pushups later.

Gary Overman has been talking since they started taping the mats. He's a hyper eighth-grader that could be a surprise force at one-fourteens. A longtime gymnast, he picks up wrestling fast with the good body control he has, control that disappears when he isn't doing something. Then his arms flail, his head bobs and his hair flops. From his mouth an unrelenting stream of consciousness issues. Everyone is used to it now. It's background noise. Well, some of the time. He's wearing Cardsen out. He's wearing everyone out. It's all the big and bitter Austin Reichs can do to keep from attacking him, grunting whenever Overman gets wound up. Overman's voice is three times louder than he thinks it is. Overman adopted Eric Lofton, and sits next to him everyday bombarding his innocent teammate with a relentless breath.

Lofton stares straight ahead, trying to ignore the incessant noise in his right ear. He groans once as he bends over to stretch.

"You're still sore after two weeks?" (no answer) "Wow, not me, not me. I feel tight like in a good way, you know strong, like in a good way? And like I do more pushups at home. I do, seriously, and I wasn't even freaking tired after running yesterday. Did you see that girl that just walked by over there? There. Over there. She just spun around, like dancing, then bent over. Bent right over. Coach, Coach, Coach, are we going to do spin drills today?" (no answer) I wonder if she'd do spin drills with us, ha, Coach, did you see her? (no answer, and now a notch quieter, Overman's version of a whisper, audible to three-quarters of the room) "For me it's just my nuts you know? Yeah, my nuts are sore like. Not *have* sores, I mean *are* sore. The right one I guess, really so..."

Cardsen explodes. His voice shakes the room.

"Overman! To the corner, twenty five P and P's! Now! And you'll make up any work you miss! Coach Waters, do you mind counting him? Thank you, each time he speaks, five more. No, not there, over there where there's no mat, maybe it'll take your sore spot away."

By now Cardsen's flash of anger is turning to a smile even as he fights to stay mad. "Anybody got anything to say about their nuts –you can join him!"

Lofton is wide-eyed. Reichs is laughing. Alan Matchik is curious. Van Gorder is red-faced. Devin is smirking and moving his head rapidly side to side to look at everyone, and Liselle Wilkins, who teaches next to Cardsen, just walked by with a stunned look, shaking her head. *Oh no.* Cardsen thinks when he sees her.

Steven Matchik, smiling wide for the first time in a long time, suddenly leaps to his feet and starts doing P and P's. "Coach, I'm sore there, too. Pride! Perfection!"

The room goes silent, followed by a buzz of voices. One by one, then in small groups, they all rise up. "Me too!" "I'm real sore there, too!" "Yeah, me, too!"

Soon all thirty five of them are crying "Pride!" as they leap into the sky throwing their arms up, "Perfection!" as they drop to their chests on the mat. Then back up fast to do it again, twenty-five times.

P and P's are part of team life under the Braxton coaches; universally applied for conditioning, getting the team's attention, building unity, and punishment. Cardsen sits in the middle looking at Steven and Steven smiles at him as he shouts and throws his arms into the air.

"Pride! Perfection!"

Now there's a kid, the Coach thinks. He sits on the mat, watching his boys go, trying not to break into a full-fledged grin. Finally, he joins them for the last fifteen.

The P and P's are just the beginning. They are now up to three sets of thirty push-ups, sit-ups, and deep knee bends and another set of "exotic" push-ups and stomach work. Basic stretches, stances and motion, neck strength, stand-ups from the mat, and takedown shots inserted between each set of strength work. The coaches do all or most of it alongside the kids as they lead. Encouragement mixed with anger. Some will never get to quality. If they try, they get encouragement, if they don't, they get yelled at. For some it's easy already, which amazes the aging Cardsen and Waters. If the strong ones don't push themselves and encourage others, it's their turn to hear it. Bad cop, good cop. A coach comes unglued at a behavior, the other catches up to the kid later and they quietly define what happened and how to change.

Skills are next. On their feet, they drill double legs with multiple finishes, single legs, high crotches and fireman's carries. The wrestlers get yelled at if they try to slip a headlock in before the other skills. That will cost a guy a match when it counts, relying on a headlock, even if he thinks he is good at it. For defense, they sprawl, push the head down and shuck, front headlock and squeeze the piss out of them, cross-faces bring the blood from noses and lips. Blood on the mat means procedures need to be followed for clean up. Braxton's eager manager, Katie Gutierrez, volunteers for that duty which secretly bewilders the coaches. On the mat it is chop-breakdowns, spirals, ankles, near cradles, power half nelson turns, cross-face cradles and chicken wings. They fight the power half, look away and peel. They fight to their knees. Reverse with stand-ups, sit-outs, switches, side rolls. No crazy hook and rolls. Only Foster Middle School does that ridiculous move.

One move per day is added in each situation until they have enough to survive a match. For the rest of the season they won't go much further than that, but rather get better at the skills they have, adding a few nuances here and there. Everyone is trained to resist so the other wrestler can complete the move, but has to work to do it. Then the roles reverse. What looks like chaos is choreography. The coaches prowl, interrupt to demonstrate, demand imitation, and stay as long as there is hope of progress, then off to another pair. No one can hide. Partners switch, coaches move in a flurry to build better match-ups, and they keep going.

Then there is live wrestling; two to four matches with varying lengths. Steven Matchik works over Ryan Van Gorder even though he gives away eleven pounds to him. The coaches take turns wrestling Alfred Rice, who is two hundred sixteen pounds on a decent frame, but still only an eighth grader. They beat on Rice, allow him to work to reversal and return the favor. They do the same with Austin Reichs, who is close to one hundred sixty. Devin Thomsen pounds on Eric Lofton. They'll have to find him better match-ups in the future. Alan Matchik is finding the groove working with Lonny Parks, who might work out at one-o-two's. In the one hundred thirties and forties two starting backs from the football team, Derek Oreste and Thomas Manzanares, work over two green but strong seventh graders.

Hall sprints. It's one hundred and five yards from music to art in Braxton Junior High. Cardsen calls for ten sprints, but when he and a number of kids nearly collapse after six, he cuts it to eight. He wonders what he'll do five years from now when he's forty-two.

They gather on the mats diving in face first to the center, pounding their hands on the mats and it sounds like hard rain. Everyone is completely soaked through with the sweat they've given up.

Cardsen steps in to the middle. "How many feel a different body than three weeks ago? How many feel their strength coming in?"

The response is a unanimous shout.

Liselle Wilkins again walks by the cafeteria where the mats are out and shakes her head. *Damn, will she just go home?* Cardsen's thoughts shout at him, but he continues on.

5

Papers scattered everywhere, an American History research project not going well. Led Zeppelin, Physical Graffiti on the CD. Three times Steven pushed 'back' to hear "Kashmir" again. He loved that old stuff. The computer glowed in the corner but Steven lay on his back on the floor. Under the bed he could see Ruff, the stuffed dog he slept with until near the end of sixth grade when a friend spotted it and laughed at him. Now it was under his bed, like he'd forgotten about it. Stored in such a way that Ruff wouldn't get thrown away, but where he could see it when he lay on his back on the floor. He rolled his head up and saw the model car he built with his dad in first grade, two baseball team photos; lame teams. On the wall, a picture torn out of the People magazine at the doctor's office, a new actress named Jessica Alba, nineteen years old, on some show in tights. He felt a shiver when he looked at her and scratched himself, a little more than necessary for scratching. To his left he saw the big poster board bracket of the district wrestling championship, Area Champion as a seventh grader. His medal hung from one of the nails that held up the bracket. For a moment he recalled running to the stands to leap into his parents' arms. He smiled when he saw for the thousandth time that he pinned Lewis out of Foster Middle in 1:56.

"You little fucker."

Steven startled so hard that he thought his muscles would rip his ribcage apart. Part of him knew immediately what was going on, the other part reeled, fear and flight from the sound, sinister beyond anything he'd heard in his young life. He was sitting up now, involuntarily. His mother filled half the doorway, disheveled in a general way, but without specifics in clothes, hair or makeup, all still intact by upper middle class standards. She looked ruined. She reached the stereo power button with her left hand and shut it off, then returned to lean against the doorframe. Her right hand brought the glass of zinfandel up so hard that some splashed out and she hit her lower lip before finding her mouth.

Was that it? Was that all? Steven rolled over and came up to his knees. "What did you say?"

"You little fucker. You covered for him. Their 'big climb' at Rainier." She snorted, took another sloppy pull. "How about butt-piloting at a cheap motel in Chehalis. You knew for a long time. So does that mean you're queer too? Faggot-gene central here? Like that?" She bobbed her head toward his championship bracket.

"Don't talk to me like that." He found himself standing now. Five foot three, but as wiry and cut as someone could be at one hundred and ten pounds. He was shaking, goose bumps up, disbelieving that after the big news, the family meeting, the counseling intervention, the soul-searching, the tears together and apart, this. "I didn't know. I didn't even know what that was, I mean, how it works... between people, I mean that it could be people like us."

She shook her head. "You know I put him through school."

"You've told us a thousand times in the last three weeks."

"You're just like him."

A spike of hurt went through him. "Get out." He moved toward her but stopped short.

"You little fucker." She looked right at him when she said it.

He shoved her once, not his hardest, but some of the wine spilled, and she was out of the doorway. Her whole body spasmed as if crying, but she was smiling.

27

"I didn't know. You knew. You laid under him for fifteen years. Don't say I knew. You knew." He shut the door and slumped to the floor. Just breathing, everything else frozen.

An hour later, Alan came knocking.

"Did she come to your room, too?" Steven asked.

"No. I went downstairs though. She made us lunches for tomorrow."

"You're perfect, right Alan? At least to her." Steven knew his brother was there to comfort him, to help him, but he quashed it anyway.

Alan looked down and didn't respond to the challenge and when he spoke he stayed with what he wanted to talk about. "Is she going nuts?"

"Going? Jesus. Have you been growing up here?" Steven saw Alan's eyes go to the floor and break contact with him.

Alan stammered a bit when he spoke. "What did she say to you?"

"Bunch of crap about Dad's money and all that."

"Oh. Well. Ok. Guess I'll see you in the morning." Alan turned to leave, moping, but turned back at Steven's voice.

"Alan, you better be sure to make ninety-sixes. You've got to be there. I think you can win a lot there."

Alan spun around. "Yeah, I think I can too. Man, I reversed that new guy, Devin, twice yesterday during live."

Alan stood hands on his hips, Steven flopped sideways on his bed, and neither one realized they were both smiling. "I hope so, you're bigger than him."

"He knows stuff, and he's tough."

"He'll make you better. He looks crazy."

"Brutal practice today! Is Cardsen insane? Three live matches, sprints, and spin drills, are you kidding me?"

"He's not insane. Well, maybe close. But yeah, I'm tired as hell. Go to bed."

Steven finally began to drift off, his body so wrung out from practice that even his racing mind couldn't fight it any more. Then he heard his mother scratching at his door like a ghoul from a horror movie, sobbing and crying, apologizing over and over and begging and crying his name. But he fell asleep anyway and she never came in even though there was no lock on the door.

6

Most of the twenty-eight students in the class had been done with the test for a long time. They stared into space, read, did extra credit reports on science magazines, or worked on other classes. For an excruciating fourteen minutes, Cardsen stared at the three people not yet finished.

Leila Charlton, certainly not dumb, measured every move, every breath, deliberate like the guy in the old westerns handling the nitro-glycerin. Analyzing the nuance of each multiple choice question, exploring every twist of the lab description, reworking each problem three times. Her brow furrowed under shoulder length, caramel-colored hair. Cardsen considered how she'd be at forty, stalled out in her engineering career, immobilized by the virtual cobwebs of the minutia of her assignments. He imagined Leila rubbing permanent lines on her forehead, watched by the boss staring out through the windows of his or her office. *For the love of God! Just bring me the report!*

If it was just her, Cardsen could have tactfully moved her to the pod to finish. Brett Walters sat next to her, trying to play cat and mouse with the teacher. He could have been done six minutes before, but he left some blank and was biding his time to get glimpses of Leila's paper when she flipped back for yet another check.

He must think I'm an idiot, thought Cardsen. I decided three minutes ago what grade he will get on those unfinished problems. His score will be exactly the same no matter what his answers are. Brett can't possibly match Leila's meticulousness, so if he uses part of her answers he will find a lot of red comments about neatness and clarity. If he uses his own explanations at this late hour, I will criticize their incompleteness. At just the right moment, Cardsen made full eye contact with Brett, blocking his fifth attempt to glimpse number 14.

Ah, the justice! No sense disrupting the quiet with an accusation and unwinnable argument, thought Cardsen, patting himself on the back.

A moment later, he was bored with that situation and thought of the third point of the triangle of still-working students, Jeremiah Bean. Another Bean. Fifth Bean that sat in that seat in nine years, each one struggling mightily with Physical Science. The laws of nature remained as foreign to the Beans as the birds of their ostrich farm were to the Oregon rain, Bean's Used RV's and Ostrich Farm. I really need to visit there sometime, mused Cardsen.

Cardsen watched another triangle from the high stool behind the demonstration desk. On the left, up front, he felt the gaze of Devin Thomsen's light blue eyes on him. When Cardsen would glance over they cast down to the desk. Cardsen looked at his test when he handed it in. Devin showed intelligence in his problem-solving but used a child's handwriting and always cut answers short.

Devin held his hands interlocked on his table. His chair pushed far back from his desk so he could lean his body forward and rest his chin on his hands. Eyes spied and hid through long, ragged bangs. The table in front of him shook from the furious pumping up and down of his knees. Devin's face remained impassive and the glimpses of his eyes showed only a cold stare that looked completely calm.

Katie Gutierrez, in the back row, represented the apex of this triangle. She pretended to be progressing on the latest Harry Potter novel. When Cardsen looked to the unfinished kids, or to Devin, her brown eyes darted over to Steven Matchik. A week before, Cardsen began to notice her concern for Steven whenever he appeared down. As wrestling manager, she had been watching him at practice. Cardsen taught her the rules. He enjoyed her help and attitude. Katie had been a fun student in his class since the beginning, and he had welcomed her when she expressed her interest in helping the team. If Steven and Katie had ever spoken to each other, Cardsen hadn't seen it.

Cardsen recalled the autobiography Katie wrote for her Spanish class. Her teacher posted it on the school website.

I am proud to be a third-generation Mexican-American. My grandparents picked apples in Washington, and my dad was born there. He is the oldest of four children. My grandparents were impressed by how much my father loved school. They joined him there, becoming the custodians of the same school. My dad graduated and went to college for a while, now he is Assistant Plant Manager at Hyster Forklifts. I am not big and I am not small, and I have long black hair. I love sports and value staying in shape. I run the 400 for the track team and I hope to win the district this year.

For a time Cardsen considered Katie, his attractive wrestling manager. The boys could not see past the scar of her cleft palate repair. She lived in an age where male scrutiny of her in late-night conversations paid irrational attention to society's definition of beauty.

To the right, Steven kept his head buried in his elbows down on his desk, hands wrapped around the back of his head, his fingers in short, curly black hair. He ground his forehead into the top of the table, as if trying to push something clear out of the back of his head. He would be in tears, the way he had been four times in the last two weeks. Cardsen wondered if Steven would stay after the bell like he did last time, with this class ending just before the lunch period.

Probing had not revealed much, either in class or at practice. The kid would only say that things were not going well at home and that he was tired. Yet Steven was still wrestling like a fiend, and with the first match coming up, looked to be ready for anything that could be out there.

The bell ended class. Everyone bolted for lunch. Devin stalled enough to get a look from Cardsen, and he returned the eye contact.

"See you at practice Devin."

"I'll see you there, Coach." He bounded out as if he just had an injection of energy.

Katie stalled as well and stole another glance at Steven, who hadn't moved and whose face remained out of sight. "Ah um, do you need me at practice Mr. Cardsen?"

"It would be great, two more wrestle-offs for varsity. You can time the matches."

She shuffled toward the door, the other students gone down the hall, then stopped and looked back at Steven.

Cardsen had followed, and he lightly touched her shoulder to get her attention. "It'll be all right." His voice was barely audible.

She nodded and moved on.

Cardsen pulled up a chair to the other side of Steven's work table. "Steven. Whatever it is, it's not getting any better. I looked at your test. I've thought back over the last two weeks of class. I'm losing you fast in here."

He raised his head and pulled his hands away. His eyes were bloodshot and his face wet. "My parents are insane."

"Big things going on?"

Steven's mouth closed tight as if to stop anything from escaping, and he nodded.

"Is your family taking counseling or anything?"

He shrugged his shoulders. "Sort of. It's kind of on hold."

"You can talk to me about it if you want. Or not. That's fine, too. You can hang out here through lunch, if you need that."

The door flew open and Liselle Wilkens came in fast. She saw what was up, and spun around and darted out with a wave when Cardsen looked at her.

"Steven, you have to understand that I might need to communicate with others because it's my job responsibility. I can talk to a counselor like Mrs. Cummings and she can talk to you more and with your folks. Or else I can to talk to your parents myself."

There was a pained attempt at a laugh. "That would be a mistake. Please don't."

"Look, Steven, I met your parents last year at Back to School Night and at a couple of our matches. Maybe if an outside person reminded them of what it has been like for you here some better things might happen."

"My Dad's gone. He lost his mind and left. My Mom has lost her mind, too, but she stayed. That's about it." Steven crossed his arms and broke eye contact. He spoke in a quiet monotone. "I can't get to sleep at night. She paces in the hall by my room. Alan wakes up a lot and runs around. Please, I'll be fine this afternoon, I promise, if I can stay here and rest a bit. Please, don't call. Give me a couple more days and if I'm still like this you can call her. Please, Coach."

Cardsen was silent, processing all the cues. "Stay here clear through lunch if you want. I can't make any promises except that any communication would only be between those who need to know, no one else. Remember this, Steven. School can be a good place to put stuff into the back of your mind and find some joy. If you are dealing with crisis and pain all the time at home, maybe school could be like a vacation sometimes. People really like you here. I see a great student when you choose to be one. What a leader you are at wrestling. The guys look to you to see how to respond to challenge. Braxton Junior High won't solve the problems, but it will keep you moving forward even if you don't realize it."

Steven nodded a couple of times. Cardsen pulled everything he could out of deep and distant places in his experience, groping. *Help me God.* He was glad that nothing here would be fake. Steven Matchik was someone Cardsen loved having around. Someone he thought about a lot, in school and out. "Steven, did you know that working with you is one of the things that makes my job fun every day? If things slipped away, academics, athletics, it would be horrible. But if you slipped away as someone I enjoy knowing, that would be even worse."

Steven looked up and tried to speak, but instead nodded once.

Cardsen stepped out in the hall. Blocking his way forward was Liselle.

"Sean. What are you doing to these kids? Trying to get them ready for a blitzkrieg?"

"Liselle..."

"Come on, look at that kid in your room. Your boot camp, or whatever it is, is crushing him."

He put his hand up. "You know me better than that. You've been right here for six years. Come on, you're not around the whole time. I mean the effect is holistic. Please don't judge on one little thing you see. You don't know anything about that boy in there."

"Holistic?" Her voice betrayed her outrage at Cardsen's blasphemy of a quality New Age term. "It's fascist. What you do with your protégés."

"Whoa. Liselle, that came out of left field. Not to mention it may be the stupidest thing I've ever heard."

"Sean, we've worked together a long time and shared a lot. You've taught me a lot. We've been friends when it counted. That's why I'm saying you just seem too close to your work, and I'm not sure what you are doing now. These boys, it's like they are all ready to be troops for you or something."

Cardsen walked by her, answering as he went, and he never looked back. "Go back to Eugene, Liselle, do another couple of years of grad school. Hell, you've got plenty of time on your hands."

Cardsen fought to ignore everything he heard from Liselle. He would bury it, destroy it, just keep working.

Down the hall he saw a worthy distraction, David Fischer, the orchestra director. Cardsen sped up and caught him.

"Sean, hey what's up?"

"Do you know a kid named Eric Lofton?"

"Of course I know Lofton. His hand is always up in the air, waving in my face. How could I not know Lofton?"

"I've been meaning to come by your room. Do you have a copy of the song 'Hoe Down,' with maybe some guitar chord letters on it?"

Fischer laughed and grabbed Cardsen by the tricep.

"Let's go get it."

7

"Dad, Tanya is going on the Honor Walk!" Cory shouted in his toddler's voice. Cardsen tossed his gym bag to the middle of the living room floor just in time for Cory's rush and picked his son up high. Tanya was right behind.

"The Honor Walk? No way."

"It's true! It's true, Dad. My turtle project got picked for display, and my behavior was the best in first grade this week!"

Cory squirmed and Cardsen released him to the floor. He ran away to leap on to the couch and pound across the cushions.

"Hey, whoa there, Cory!"

Tanya stood with one hand on a hip, a six year old posed like some diva waiting to be further acknowledged. Cardsen smiled at her and kissed Tanya on the forehead on his way in to the kitchen. "I'm so proud of you!"

A pot of spaghetti and a pan of sauce steamed on the stove. Sonia met him for a kiss.

"Wow, this is like some show from the fifties! Thanks for cooking."

"The kids have been a big help. What else can we do? The rain is here to stay. It's that time of year already."

"Pretty cool about Tanya."

"You should have seen her come off the bus. She ran across to me without a look at the street."

"Do you have to go back in tonight?"

"I ran all my therapies today. Scheduling has been smooth and I doubt we'll do evenings at the hospital for a while. So, it's working out good for this time of year. Although I suppose we could use the hours, moneywise."

"Forget it. We'll be fine. Do you have to rush to get Cory and meet Tanya?"

"You know I-84. It's takes twenty minutes to get a half a mile to the highway, and then sixteen to get all the way out here."

"Glad we had a good summer, Sonia, because I'm buried August to Christmas."

"That's what summer is for I guess. But Sean, it's getting harder every year, you know?"

"Yeah, I know."

"How's practice?"

"Kicking my butt. I think we're going to be pretty tough. You know, Abe Lincoln over in Gresham will be good, but it's hard to imagine many others standing up to this crew. I've been waiting a long time for a team like this. Steven Matchik, he's a beast. And this new kid, Devin, wait until you get a look at him. You should see Alfred at heavyweight. Man, he's come so far." Cardsen went to sip some spaghetti sauce from the wooden spoon sticking out of it.

"Ryan Van Gorder, that amazing Mormon kid I talk about, he can do it again this year. We've got a little guy that's sixty-eight pounds to wrestle seventy-fives. Elia Azan, kid's Egyptian. Sometimes I wonder if he's really supposed to be in seventh grade. But I worry about the eligibility list, it might get ugly for this quarter. That could derail us. Outside of Ryan, we've got every flunker, outlaw, emotionally disturbed kid you can imagine."

"How is Steven doing? Isn't he the one you said has started to stay and cry?"

"Shaky at school. Freakishly good at wrestling. But I am worried he could come apart. I mean, he couldn't leave my room the other day for an hour. At the match, I've got to corner his mom or dad. I tried to call, but couldn't get anyone and I didn't want to leave a message for Steven to intercept."

"Tanya's program's Tuesday."

"I'll come right after the match, hopefully not too late."

***

The team moves like colorful ants on the black mats, jumping the seams together and pulling tight across it with a partner. Others crawl under them, running the tape. Some of the wrestlers imagine themselves to be in charge, but the big gym swallows their high-pitched shouts. The scorekeeper fiddles with the cords to the scoreboard controls, accidentally setting off the obnoxious buzzer several times. The custodians pull the last accordion stands out. Other wrestlers straighten the chairs that will hold the opposing teams on opposite sides of the mat.

Cardsen barks a few orders but is generally pleased with the set-up, the older kids proud to take charge. He rechecks his paperwork in his coach's chair near the edge of the mat. Simultaneously, Cardsen pulls in data on the team members, how they work, how prepared they look, if they screw around. Katie Gutierrez and Steven Matchik are about to converge, and he plays with his papers, secretly watching them.

Katie follows upright behind the wrestlers on their knees taping mat sections together, sweeping a wet mop side to side. She is startled when Steven is suddenly beside her. His arms are swinging in circles, he's bouncing on his toes. He won't stop moving until this match is over. It's the closest he's ever stood to her and she gets nervous.

And then he speaks. "You don't have to do the mopping."

"I kind of like it."

"You can't let these guys think all you do is serve us. It isn't right."

She can't look at him and she keeps swabbing.

39

"You know Katie, people can serve you, too. Let me take it."

He calls her by name. He grabs the handle, the motion showing cords in his forearm. Questions fill her eyes about the meaning of his approach, an adolescent world on fire. He smiles at her and she is able to play it cool. She smiles back. "It's all yours, Steven." She yields and puts her hand on her hips. Then he's mopping with his back to her and moving away.

The team from Sunnydale walks in with numbered sky-blue hooded sweatshirts and sweatpants, carrying old style plastic headgear. Cardsen clears half the mat space for them, and goes over to talk with the opposing coach. "Hey Jimmy. Looks like you got a full team." Cardsen shakes his hand.

"It's been a stretch Sean, but I've scraped a full lineup together. I'm not sure some of these guys have a Y chromosome. You might have to take it easy on me like you did when we got in that fight in college. I'm lucky you didn't kill me."

"Aw, come on, Jimmy, you always bring that up. You would have kicked my ass if you hadn't drunk all those shots."

"Maybe I would have. Stop smiling Sean, it makes me nervous. Hey, are you helping with the East Side Clinic this year?"

"Naw, the season is about all I can do anymore with the family. Plus, that guy from Gladstone will be there. All the coaches are fun and we get that one jerk."

"Yeah, I know. It's not football or basketball, we're all supposed to be cool to each other."

"It is different in wrestling, isn't it? You know, after tonight, maybe we get the teams together and have a joint practice down the road."

"Yeah, I'd love to. But we always say we will, and then we get too busy. Is the ref here?"

"He is. Let's weigh in about twenty minutes from now."

"Perfect."

Settled once again to his coaching chair, Cardsen glances back and sees that the Braxton wrestling team's new addition has started in on some work. Evidently it will not be a short session. Cardsen watches amazed as, one by one, Devin Thomsen takes all the smaller guys back to the practice mat behind the chairs and pounds them with moves. He slams them into cradles or puts a leg in and turks them and cranks their heads until they make noises of pain. He chokes them in front headlocks and throws them down hard on takedowns. After each brief and vicious pounding they beg off and he goes for another kid to invite back. First Eric Lofton and two JV ninety pound wrestlers, then Alan Matchik, Gary Overman, and now he finds Lonnie Parks.

This has to stop, but it's just too entertaining. The kid's inner motor must be running a thousand miles an hour, running out of control, nothing seems to take the edge off for this kid. No, Braxton hasn't seen much of this. Let's see where it leads.

The teams are called to the locker room. Coach Waters is waiting for Cardsen there.

"How we looking Matt?"

"Just fine. I haven't seen anyone overweight. Alan was close, but we just checked and he'll be fine."

"Thanks, Matt. Let's get the rest of them stripped down."

The varsity wrestlers strip to their underwear, or naked if they are close on weight. From 75 pounds, where Elia Azan steps up looking like a fakir who lost his clothes, to heavyweight Alfred Rice, who dwarfs the stocky referee moving the scale, the wrestlers will come one by one. Some, like Steven Matchick and Austin Reichs, show their athleticism in every move they make. Others, like Devin Thomsen, are still so small that it's hard to reconcile their muscularity with their size. Mostly they are typical kids, some carrying an embarrassing roll around the middle, others have sticks for arms. Rookies like Eric Lofton are shy about the whole scene. Others should be, judging by the way they handle themselves, literally. In about half the cases their ability matches their appearance; there are weak looking kids that wrap their opponents like constrictor snakes, short fat kids that are impossible to get on their back, and a few that look like Tarzan but wrestle like Jane.

Devin's weight is called. He steps up and stands upright, chest out. He brings something with him, an aura that quiets those that he walks by; something different that no one could explain. Cardsen notices the constant twitch in the kid's fingers; he's wound so tight that Cardsen searches for something to give the kid some kind of relief. Devin makes weight and looks up at Cardsen.

Cardsen gives him a big smile. "Welcome aboard Thomsen, you're going to do great. You're ready, son."

Devin smiles his first genuine smile of the day. He's heard every word the way it should be heard, including the last word, which Cardsen has already forgotten saying.

Gary Overman steps up to weigh in at one-hundred-fourteen pounds. His opponent is a young softie, an obvious fill-in for Sunnydale because there was no one else. If there is any potential at all, it's a couple of years from being visible. In deference to the slaughter everyone knows is coming, the coaches and kids from both teams are almost always very supportive, sure to congratulate and encourage. In wrestling the end will be quick on the mat, if not merciful.

Overman has been muttering, whispering to others, rubbing his eyes, whistling, grabbing his parts, pulling his underwear up tight and laughing at himself. His usual stream continues as he steps up. "So this is it I guess. Yeah, should make it, huh coach?

(no answer) I'll step up, won't trip, not like Eric, hey Eric, nice trip."

The referee is a bit perturbed and his voice is tight. "Young man, step off and wait until I set your weight class on the scale and I say step up."

"Yes sir! Guess you got to have the weight right on there, but really, it will be no problem. One-hundred-fourteen, yep, one one four."

"Overman, shut your mouth." There is a seriousness in Cardsen's voice that even Overman can't ignore. Overman makes weight and as he steps off glances back at his opponent then at Cardsen.

"Hey Coach, did you see my guy? He has tits. Tits!"

The room goes silent. Cardsen can't be ready for everything. When he finally emerges from the shock he's out from behind the scale and sticks the edge of his clipboard hard into Overman's chest. The veins exploding out of the coach's forehead overrule any psychological label that might allow for Overman's lack of self-control. "Damn it Overman, shut it right now or you're going home. Get your ass back there and put your uniform on." Cardsen was loud as usual and the locker room reverberates with echoes. Overman recoils through the locker room from Cardsen's furious approach, right into Coach Waters. Waters marches Overman into the coaches' office for what Cardsen knows will be a more detailed verbal flogging. The kid from Sunnyvale weighs in. No one can look at the kid now, not even the ref.

8

Steven leads the Braxton wrestling team in an explosion out of the locker room door as the speakers in the gym launch into Guns n' Roses' "Welcome to the Jungle." Katie starts the song at just the right moment. They've left their sweatshirts behind and are in camouflage T-shirts with "Welcome to the Jungle" printed in orange. They circle the mat for their final five minute warm-up routine. Ryan Van Gorder, their other defending area champion, joins Steven in the center to help lead.

The stands are small but they are packed with kids and parents. The student section holds up painted signs with camouflage backgrounds: Welcome to the Jungle, Braxton Zoo, Matchik=Magic. Steven tries not to stare at the sign that bears his name. The cheers are a shriek above the loud music. Alan looks nervous. He scans the stands end to end. *No, Alan, our parents are not here.* Steven won't say that out loud. The drawn order put Alan's match last, but Steven knows their parents will still be absent at that time.

Ryan Van Gorder's joyous family, two parents and five siblings, an effective advertisement for the Latter Day Saints, take up a visible segment of the stands. Alfred Rice's mom and dad take up nearly the same sized segment with just the two of them. The students are rowdy and excited to see what the rumors are about, that Braxton's lineup is stacked all the way.

The one-hundred-two weight class starts and Lonny Parks in his first varsity match gets a quick double leg takedown, hoisting his man high before bringing him down, and the crowd senses blood. Parks cruises, scoring at will. Toward the end of the second period he pins his opponent by overpowering him with a cross-face cradle. The crowd is up and the slaughter is on.

Steven is the second match. His opponent is talented, a runner-up the year before in a weight class different than Steven's. Steven moves side to side, fakes a single-leg and backs out. He ties the head briefly, moving the kid in a circular fashion, and so fast half the crowd misses it, ankle-picks the leg that has moved forward. He nearly pins the kid there but his opponent doesn't quit and surprises by slipping out behind for a reversal.

Not here, not now. No one takes this away from me. This is my house. This is all I am. They have a sign with my name on it. I'm alone and I'm on stage, they can't see what this means, they can't know. How could they? I don't even know why I do what I do. But this kid, he can't touch me. I am going to tear him apart. He will remember who took him apart.

Second period. Steven starts down. A perfect switch and he is riding, pounding the arms to pull in chicken wings. Cardsen is yelling to watch his hips and stay behind the arms. Steven lacks patience to stay back, and the kid sits out to face Steven. Both wrestlers are on their knees, head-tied for just a moment before Steven Matchik short headlocks him with a vicious slide of his forearm across the face. It's over eight seconds later.

He hugs Coach Waters on the way off and then he's shaking Coach Cardsen's hand, who wraps his other arm around his captain.

"That was an awesome start to the year. I'm proud of you. Let's work on not getting out of control."

"Coach, I just want to kill everyone."

"Be a wrestler *and* a fighter. Don't forget your skills."

And then it's on to the next kid. Braxton wins eight of the next twelve matches, five by pins. Eric Lofton is the only one that has been pinned by Sunnydale, but the coaches see to it that he is fully honored by the team on the way off the mat.

Steven looks to the scoreboard. 52-15. Devin is the next match, and then Alan. Steven studies Devin as he warms up. *That's a wrestler for sure.* He looks to the rest of the team, turned away from Lofton to look at Devin, just as excited about what might come next.

9

Devin bounced on the practice mat, heart about to burst out of his chest, when he saw his mother come in the far door with his sisters. She held Leza's hand and tugged at Kimmy's upper arm to help her along. Like she always did. Like that day in June. He ran through it all again, while he was bouncing, sweat pouring from his hair down his back.

***

Something about the way the car skidded in front of the house made Devin jump. He'd seen it before: Cracker's car. A big rusted boat. His sisters were near the back door on their way in to find something to eat. He saw his mother lean out the back door and seize Kimmy by the upper arm to pull her in. When men came out of all four doors and slammed them harder than normal, the hackles went up on the back of his neck. Devin threw one more dirt clod at the old shed. Seven of ten previous throws hit home and this clod went true and exploded against the door.

Someone might have to help Mom and Dad talk to Cracker. Devin had heard some things, seen some things. They might take everything they had left, like the TV or his bike or the cool book about Vietnam his teacher gave him. His sisters didn't know how to stay out of the way. Devin sprinted for the back door. The back screen hung only from its bottom hinge and it held him up for a second.

Tense laughter came from the kitchen, along with Roy's voice. Roy had been his dad for as long as he could remember. Sometimes he forgot there was some other dad, one he never met.

"Come on, have a beer with me, please just drink one. Let me think, and we can talk. I mean, my family's here."

"Four beers. You got four beers? How do you afford four beers? And them smokes? Shit, I don't even got smokes. Maybe you got some of my shit in the freezer?"

Cracker opened the refrigerator giving Devin a sharp glance as he arrived at the kitchen.

The men filled the small kitchen. Devin recognized two of them, Lloyd and Jack. They both looked at him, sad like, then looked away. The fourth man seemed huge compared to his companions and Devin's scrawny dad. A few times he'd snuck out of his room and watched them howl late at night, his dad and these men, when they'd come in from wherever.

"Aw, Roy, you got all kinds of stuff in here. Like five beers and some boloney. Man, don't you know your kids got to eat? You're pathetic. You got to get your shit together." Cracker pulled a can of beer from the refrigerator. He glanced out into the living room.

Devin also looked out and saw his mom grabbing at his squirming sisters, shushing them and wrestling to hang on to four year old Kimmy's upper arm.

"Wish I had me a hole to drink with like Alexa. You've seen her drink, boys. She can pack it away. I know she packs in other ways. Remember '89, Alexa? Before this clown came along?"

"Screw you, Cracker!"

"That's what I'm talking about."

Roy took one step forward and Cracker smashed the beer from the refrigerator so hard into his face that it exploded, showering everyone in the kitchen with Hamm's. Roy went backward into the small table and chairs, blood from his split forehead already spilling down over his nose. He flailed with his arms and legs, knocking over another chair as he tried to stand and failed.

Devin's stomach leapt into his throat. He looked to the living room at his mother.

"Devin, let's go!" His mom was dragging the girls by their arms toward the door with her head twisted back at the partition.

Jack and another man went out the other entrance to the kitchen, around the short hall, and caught up to her, blocking her path.

Then a big hand gripped Devin's upper arm.

Alexa and all three kids were put on the couch together, eyes wide with terror. The girls sniffled and wiped snot out of their hair. Jack and Lloyd, their longtime friends, stayed in front of the couch after forcing them down. The Big Man blocked the front door. Soaked with blood, Roy sat on a chair brought out from the kitchen, holding a washcloth to his forehead.

Cracker had a large, green automatic pistol. "Come on Roy, I turned half that shit over to you. I need answers. I trusted you. You owe me. Where did it all go? Rails is going to do this to me, what I'm doing to you, only it will be a lot worse. I got to deliver him money Roy. Roy, where's the money? Where'd it go?"

"Four days. Cracker, come on, I'll sell everything I got, everything in this house. I'm waiting on these guys from Portland to pay. They can't come out because they're under surveillance."

Cracker shook his head as he listened to the slurred speech out of Roy's lips, red with the blood that had flowed down from his head. Cracker pushed the barrel of the gun into the soft part of Roy's cheek. "Guys from Portland? No. You snorted as much as you could handle. Remember, you picked up Jack and said the party was on? Then you took some more, gave a lot away. No one from Portland. It's either here, Roy, or you let it slip back to some of Rails' wetbacks to hide. I haven't had a blow in weeks. I got nothing left. I practically live in a goddamn box, and Rails is going to kill me, not hit me with a goddamn beer."

Cracker moved to the couch and pointed the gun at Kimmy. Alexa moved to cover her but Lloyd grabbed Alexa by the hair and pulled her to the floor, crying in pain, as the Big Man took her arms behind her.

When Devin tightened and started to rise, Jack kicked him hard in the knee with a boot, blinding his mind with hot light, pain and fear.

"Five seconds, Roy."

"I can't let you in Cracker! They'll kill me!" Roy cried.

"Kill you? I'm probably going to do that. Better worry about today more than tomorrow."

"You won't kill me or you won't get it."

"But this little bitch of yours..." Cracker's voice was shaky now. Then he raised his gun up and away from Kimmy. "Boys, I can't kill a little girl. I don't think I can."

There was a pause as everyone waited. There were snorts and miserable moans from Alexa as she struggled against Lloyd's tightened grip on her long hair. Whimpers came from the girls. Devin saw it all through a bee's multiple eyes. He saw each person and their agony clearly, individually.

Cracker heaved a deep breath and then grabbed Devin by the hair, and dragged him out on the carpet. "Get on your knees."

The gun barrel rested on the top of his front lip. The tall snout of the automatic pushed his nose up. Devin's eyes crossed a bit. Then he refocused. Cracker's hairy arm. Pale white skin, black hair. It looked dead. He smelled their house for the first time in a long time; urine and stale dog shit and beer and rotten food. His mouth had gone dry and he recognized he was hungry. He tried to think about Heaven but he couldn't make himself care.

Devin looked up into Cracker's eyes, sunken brown holes in the man's drawn face. Cracker couldn't stand the gaze. His body jerked back and he looked away. The gun remained.

"Let him go, I'll do anything, I'll do all of you." His mother struggled to talk, and then Lloyd's hand covered her mouth.

Time slowed for Devin. He looked away from Cracker and over to Roy, visible out of one eye. Devin saw tears mixing with Roy's blood and he didn't believe those tears solely came from a gun pointed at his son's face. Exhaustion and pain contorted Roy's face. Devin counted backward. The man had been binging for eight or nine days; hardly sleeping, the house a center of coming and going. Noise, endless noise. Roy said he would leave town but then the car quit and Roy began to pace the house like a caged animal babbling about Cracker knowing this or that and no one left to call. Once he saw Devin staring at him from the corner of a doorway and screamed, *"Quit staring at me you judgmental little bastard!"* Roy bolted after him but by then the man was a wreck and Devin easily made it to the door first, staying outside for hours until things quieted down.

Had the man ever loved him? Maybe. There were laughs back in their memories somewhere, before the crank and the booze and the constant drama became the centerpiece of all they had. Roy used to work jobs. He used to put his arm around Alexa's waist even when sober. One time he took Devin fishing way out on the Columbia. Their little boat rocked in the rough waves and Roy laughed and smiled at him dismissing his fears.

But now this was the life Roy had given them.

Roy noticed Devin's eye and stared back, pressing the rag against his head harder and snorting snot and blood. Roy shook his head. "You'll be better off. Go back to those angels that put you in your mom. You're an alien or something, not mine. You'll be better off there than here."

So that was that. Devin had seen the movies on TV. The back of his head would blow out and spray everyone, and there would be bits of brain or something stuck to the far wall. His mom would have to look at that. The girls would have to look at that. And it would be painted right there for Roy. He knew Roy would survive the night, somehow, raging on forever with coke or pills or that cowboy crank or something.

"Shut the hell up! Knock off your freaky shit, Roy."

Cracker's voice broke when he yelled and Devin could feel the barrel of the gun vibrating against the front of his nose and upper lip. Cracker wheezed a weak laugh that sounded like an old woman wearing an oxygen mask.

"Alien. Man, everyone screwed Alexa back then I guess."

"Shoot him."

Cracker turned to face Roy at the quiet words.

"I don't give a shit, he ain't mine. He ain't nobody's. Costs me a lot of money to keep around. But shooting that freak won't make me tell."

Devin heard it. He knew he should be amazed at what he heard. He should be angry. He should start to cry. Maybe he should beg so someone could be there for his sisters. But he felt nothing but the unyielding metal hard against the bone between his nostrils, and how thirsty he was, how dry his lips were. He popped his upper lip over the top of the gun barrel, and his mouth closed around it lips cooling on the steel.

Cracker felt the bump of the gun and when he turned back from Roy and looked down he saw Devin with the barrel in his mouth, eyes still up. Cracker's whole body jerked tight with some combination of revulsion and excitement. "What the...!" He jerked the pistol hard out of Devin's mouth, whole body shaking. He took a step back.

He fired the gun.

Devin went down backward from his knees, and then his legs unfurled from that awkward position. He came up on an elbow. He reached to touch his cheek with his other hand, and felt something wet. Then he gasped as his head seemed to cave in and his sight became wavy, distorted.

Cracker was jumping. Just jumping up and down in place. Roy had his eyes closed. Devin glanced back to the far wall. No brains there. He looked to the couch. His mom had vomited into Lloyd's hand. He yelled something at her as he covered her mouth. Kimmy and three year old Leza wrapped around each other on the couch, eyes buried.

Then Jack was on Cracker. He wrapped his arms around the smaller Cracker, pinning the gun tight to the shooter's side.

"Ease off, Cracker. I know how to get us cut back in. I know how. No more shooting. I'll get Roy to come through. I'll do it.

The Big Man suddenly moved. He released his grip on Alexa's arms and moved toward Jack and Cracker. As the Big Man passed him, Devin looked up at his face. The Big Man pulled his hand back, swung low and whacked him as hard as the man possibly could on the dry side of his head. Flying like a swatted housecat, he became so light. He saw the carpet coming and changing to black.

***

An eagle can soar without flapping his wings for nearly two minutes. All the while watching the thing that scurries below, eking out a living with hard work and meticulous dedication, oblivious to the fact that it is being watched. They are both part of the whole, part of God's great ecological puzzle. But when the feathers get pulled back and the furious rush of the dive is reached, beauty joins violence and there is no more moral equality among creatures. One is great, important, beautiful and lasting. The other is food.

***

Even those new to the sport noticed the way Devin moved. How could someone be so small, thin, and pale, yet so alive and ripped with strength at the same time? Long white hair hanging out his headgear, circling movement, jab-steps forward and feline sprawls back. He knifes ahead, cutting into his opponent and disappearing for just a split second. And then the other boy is airborne, a perfect fireman's carry with a jolt through the crotch and straight up that sends a body on a high-amplitude arc. There's more, but from that point on it is the details of an excruciating struggle for survival by a tough but outmatched creature and the relentlessness of a single-purpose predator.

When he comes off the mat, he is mobbed by the other kids. He looks to Cardsen, who can't get near him, and they both smile. Later, Cardsen will grab him and tell him how glad he is to have him at Braxton, and he will tell him to please, please calm down and get some sleep tonight. And Devin will sleep that night, deep and long, howls and moans way off in the distance, like they are not actually inside of him.

10

"Alan, hey, it's just a match." Steven walked over and sat in the dark living room across from Alan, who reclined in their dad's old chair. The little noises he made let Steven know that he was crying. Alan shot his arms up stiffly then brought them down to cover his face, groaning.

"How would you know? You never lose."

"You wrestled pretty well. I liked your standup."

"Standup? Like that's a big deal. Lofton got a standup. Everyone won but me. And I was the last match, too. Sends everyone out remembering it."

"We gave up eighteen points. That's four or five matches. And I didn't see anyone from that crowd leave the gym unhappy."

"It's not for me. I'll never do what you do. And that Devin Thomsen, he nearly broke my neck before the match. All season Cardsen's going to have me with that guy."

"It's one match. One match! I guarantee you place this year if you work. We need you at ninety-six."

"Mom and Dad didn't come."

"Who cares? They probably will never come again."

"How can they not watch you? You're a champion. And this was my first one ever."

"Did you really want Dad there? What if he brought..."

Steven heard Alan suck air and snot in.

"Why couldn't he have at least waited another year?"

Steven didn't have any answer.

"Mom didn't even ask us how we did when she picked us up."

"She's being honest. She doesn't care. She can bite me. Alan, there's nothing here. If you come home after school, it will suck beyond belief."

"X-box."

"Screw X-box."

As Steven walked upstairs, he fought to keep from breaking down. It was getting harder and harder. Cardsen's room at school had been the place he would get overwhelmed. Maybe he wanted Coach to see, hear Coach's voice about the subject of his family. He fought to end that desire when Coach called him out on it the last time. He couldn't bear the thought of his parents revealing all to Cardsen or of Cardsen seeing them in their pathetic glory.

Now, on his way to bed, his strength was ebbing. The incentives to hold up were fading along with the day and there was no one to see him. Steven tried to think about Jessica Alba, he tried to think about Katie Gutierrez, even though she had a weird mouth. He thought about visiting those sex websites he found last weekend. After all, no one checked up on it anymore. None of those thoughts held him up and he kept crashing. He ran through the match one more time, moment by moment in his head, and then he was in his bed, curling into himself.

11

Devin winced at Cardsen's booming voice, so loud it hurt his good ear. His left ear, the bad one, was fine. Since the shooting in June, he retained a permanent loss of hearing and all sounds seemed smooth and mellow in his left ear. He looked high up on the wall at the signs posted for the upcoming canned food drive for the poor. Would that include his family? He hoped not. How long could Cardsen's tirade go on? Devin twisted to see the clock. Seven minutes already.

"Seven guys with F's in English. Are you kidding me? Seven. Three F's in Math. Two in History and Science. If we had two matches this week and wrestled tomorrow, we'd leave eight people home. Five of you are supposed to be varsity. Oreste, what language do we speak in America?"

"English."

"That's right, English. You're flunking your own language. Now, let's see if you can understand this, ANYONE INELIGIBLE IS A NO-GOOD SUMBITCH TO THIS TEAM! What language was that Oreste?"

"English, sir. Well, most of it."

"Overman, it says here you're flunking Teen Living. How old are you?"

"Thirteen. I mean thirteen and two months. Actually I was premature, I should -"

"THAT'S RIGHT OVERMAN, THIR*TEEN.* You're flunking your age. Get this. We're Five and 0, crushing everyone, and we are going to keep winning. Either decide to be part of it or we will do it without you. Any of you."

Devin stared at his Coach. Veins popped out on the forehead of his red face. Coach hates me now. I've let us down.

He had tried to write a couple of papers. The first one was supposed to be about the things in your family history that make you proud. In the end he wrote two paragraphs about his mom's bravery; brave when she stopped drinking and got an AA sponsor when they moved here; brave when she took him to the doctor to get the grazing wound on the side of his head stitched and medicine for the eye damaged by the air blast. His mom told the doctor she was having an affair with a laborer named Hernandez who accidentally shot him while playing with a gun. In her story, he got scared and ran for Mexico, and Devin's concussion came from falling down after the shot. The police came to the doctor's office and she stuck to her story so they could leave faster. She was brave when she left no clues for Roy about where they were, on the run for months until they came here. Brave when she started working at the warehouse and did all the government paperwork for daycare and food stamps and other stuff.

But he couldn't say all that. He only wrote that she was brave for raising three kids on her own so he crumpled it up and threw it away.

The second paper was on how it would be to live like Huckleberry Finn. Deep down he knew he should have written some crap. For the team, he should have done it. But after the second time he read the book, which he found somewhat interesting, he never lifted a pencil.

"Now, get up off your asses and get ready, because you may have to crawl out of here when we are done with you!" Cardsen had boomed again.

Devin leapt to his feet without a conscious thought to do so. He grabbed a partner and set to work on his skills.

Cardsen didn't lie. Practice marched on at a relentless pace; full skills work, four sets of strength, and three full speed matches. Devin was surprised when his motor began to run down. That never happened. He could last longer than anyone in the room.

His third match was against Alan Matchik and Alan came at him with a ferocity that Devin had not seen. Tears filled Alan's angry eyes and spittle came out of the side of his mouth. They did not speak to each other. At the end, for the first time, Alan caught Devin on his back and pinned him. When the whistle blew, Devin wriggled away in shock and saw Cardsen looking at him. Devin went to a brick pillar and sat on the floor with his back to it. Cardsen still stared. Then Cardsen walked right at him, stopping where he towered above.

"Thomsen, I want to see you in the coach's office after practice." He turned and walked away.

This is it. They are done with me.

***

"How many times did we warn them, Matt? We have everyone stay together and we walk away with the championship. Just walk into it. I guess I don't know how to motivate them in the classroom. They're going down, not up."

Waters stretched his back and went to a chair in the office. "Don't let them tell you it's because they're tired. This is the most structure they ever get. Practice, home to eat and work, then bed. You and I both know they have more homework time when they live under structure."

"This team could have something together they'd never forget. Success based on work. It's disgusting; some of them are acting like lazy, pampered, suburban pricks."

"I don't think Devin Thomsen fits that, but he went down today."

"Yeah, I saw it. He's coming in here tonight."

A knock stopped them, and Ryan Van Gorder appeared in the doorway.

"I was wondering if I could talk to you about something."

Cardsen's demeanor swung away from anger and landed on a calm smile. Ryan stood in front of him in a sweater and an open raincoat, a gym bag over his shoulder, and his saxophone case in hand. His brown hair was cut tight, and he had a thoughtful look on his face. Cardsen knew he would always remember Ryan that way. He and Steven were champions as seventh graders. Steven Matchik might be the magic but Ryan Van Gorder was the glue that held the whole thing together. Not only a champion, Ryan had also been Braxton Rotary Club Student of the Year, and remained kind to stoners, minorities, shy girls and ugly boys. "Come in Ryan. Close the door."

"Coach, um, the F's in English. I wanted to talk to you about that."

Cardsen half expected to be reprimanded for his language and punitive style on the day, and the thing was, if it came from Van Gorder, he'd have to listen.

"Ok, Ryan."

"I think a lot of those grades might be from Mrs. McCall's class. It's just that, well, she has this pile of papers on her desk. It seems about two feet tall, ones she said she'd grade by like a week or two ago. I'm not saying all the guys are doing well in there, but we've only had I think four grades this quarter. So, if one is missing, you're way down already. Some of their papers might be in that giant stack, ungraded, and entered as zeros in the book. Mr. Cardsen, if I'm wrong I'll feel kind of foolish on this, but I don't think I am."

Cardsen locked his hands behind his head and nodded. "Thanks Ryan. Keep it quiet if you don't mind. It's kind of political. I'll look into it. And remember, there are plenty of bad grades outside of English, so keep encouraging the others."

When Ryan left, Cardsen noticed Waters and shook his head, smiling. "Don't say it. I should have known. Should have been on it the minute I saw six of seven were hers. She couldn't find her ass with both hands. Now I got to go down there and see if she'll acknowledge her dusty pile. Four grades. I know they do papers on books and stuff, but four grades in the gradebook? She did this same thing to us two years ago."

Devin came in next, after a light knock. The kid shuffled in, jeans and a white t-shirt intended to be an undershirt, no eye contact. His white hair covered his face and blended with his shirt, making it seem as if he had no head. Waters left to the shower and Cardsen beckoned him to sit. "Do you have a sweatshirt? It's like thirty-seven degrees and raining."

"Yes sir."

"Does your mom pick you up?"

"She will tonight."

"I want her to come in for a minute when she gets here. Do you understand?"

"Yes."

"Devin, look at me."

The kid looked up with the blue eyes that caught everyone's attention, and caused most to turn away from their intensity. But not Cardsen. Nothing about Devin Thomsen could scare him. He held eye contact with Devin. Someone had to. In his mind, Cardsen ran through what the school counselor knew. No dad. Multiple kids. On the run from abuse. Mom refused to say from where and facilitate the transfer of records. Social worker backed her. Whatever happened, mom implied Devin bore the worst of it. Cardsen felt a fire rise in him. No way was he going to lose this kid. No way.

"You've got a solid A in my Science class. You've shown progress in every way. You killed our last test. So how do I reconcile that with an F in McCall's class and now two D's? My gosh, Teen Living and Math. Same math we use in Science where you do it right all the time."

"It's just that well, um, it's that, I think I like Science."

As Devin stumbled through his only sentence, the coach got the message loud and clear. As Cardsen suspected, Devin liked the Science *teacher* and impressing him was all that mattered.

"What we like or don't like can't always be the determining factor in what we are willing to do. Do you like running halls?"

"Not too much, but I do like to run."

"We run because it makes us better, and we don't dwell a lot on whether we like it or not. Likewise, successful students work in all their classes, not just the ones they enjoy the most. How far down are you in McCall's English?"

"All the way. I have a zero."

"For the last paper?"

"For the quarter."

***

"You have an amazing son."

Alexa Thomsen sighed like a southern belle hearing a formal flattery. Tears appeared, but she forced them away. "You think so?"

"I'm around a lot of kids. I know so."

"The teachers haven't liked working with him in school. They've said he doesn't respond in a predictable manner to normal exchanges."

"Ha. What's not to enjoy? And I don't respond in a predictable manner to normal exchanges."

She laughed and tossed her hair back from her lined face. Cardsen remembered the first time he had seen her, and now he had the same impression, hard living on a fine mind and attractive features.

"Ms. Thomsen, Devin is on the verge of failing several classes. He wants to please me right now most of all. He has an A in Science and is a dominant wrestler but is sinking in everything else. Devin seems to need me in front of his face to perform. He hasn't grasped that the stuff he does away from me is even more important, and that I am pulling for him there, too."

Alexa put her head down to her hand, unable to respond. Cardsen looked out the door of the coaches' office, which he had propped open to make the conference less awkward, and watched the rain splatter against the window.

When ready she spoke in the tone of a radio newsperson. "I'm an alcoholic in recovery so if this sounds like I'm sharing at AA that's because I gave this speech there last night." Alexa managed a weak smile. "His father used drugs. It got bad and we had to go. Devin has always been in a mess at school because we didn't do the right things, didn't work with him on stuff at home. He's survived on what he's taught himself and little things about the way he operates are different than most kids. At times I've helped him, because I was a pretty good student, but now he makes bad choices to punish me if I try. I got him in a youth group at First Methodist. I loved church when I was young. He's gone twice and says he likes the stuff but doesn't fit in with the other kids."

She stretched her hands out and glanced at Cardsen. "In June, Devin was shot by a friend of his father. I'm calling it an accident –I don't answer any questions on the details. The bullet grazed Devin's head, ripped it deep, and the blast damaged the hearing in his left ear and the vision in his left eye. His eye was solid red all summer. I think his eyesight has come all the way back. There's a scar under his hair."

She gave him a bit of time to absorb. Cardsen was grateful for that. He didn't emote, offered no condescension or visible surprise. Of course inside it was different, his gut tightened and his spirit cried out. He had anger and empathy and no place to pour it out in the needed quantity. Devin would be on the mat for a few weeks and their lessons would be the only weapon against demons. As always, it was a goddamned mismatch. For a moment, Cardsen mused about how often he coached wrestlers that struggled with being impulsive. No wonder he enjoyed them, he was worse. He could swallow an emotional response and at the same instant commit himself to a lifetime of work.

Cardsen grabbed a stack of yellow post-it notes and a pen. "Ms. Thomsen, I've seen a great number of kids benefit by sticking with this sport. If Devin is going to continue to wrestle, he must write an English paper and do two response worksheets by the day after tomorrow. And then we are going to need a lot more after that. Would it be possible to set aside an hour every night for Devin to work under your supervision?"

"I can. My sponsor comes over almost every night, and we all just hang out. Devin's the only boy, so I think he gets tired of that sometimes. The television is out of the way in the back room. His sisters can pop in something on the VCR."

"This is my phone number. If he won't do his work, tell him you're going to call me. And don't hesitate – just call anytime."

After she left, Cardsen stared at the dark, wet window for a few minutes before he moved to gather his things.

Out in the parking lot Cardsen was surprised to see Matt Waters rolling down the window of his car. Cardsen leaned down to see Matt in the glow of the dash lights. "What are you doing here? You didn't have to stay."

Matt shrugged. "She could have accused you of anything in there. I could see you from here."

Cardsen smiled and shook his head. "Thanks, man. It means a lot." Cardsen thought about what Alexa told him, but he couldn't find the energy to tell the story to Matt. "Have a good night. We'll see who shows up ready to go tomorrow."

12

"When Jesus entered the ruler's house and saw the flute players and the noisy crowd, he said, 'Go away. The girl is not dead but asleep.' But they laughed at him. After the crowd had been put outside, he went in and took the girl by the hand, and she got up. Everyone thought she was dead, including her mother. But her mother had so much faith she thought she would try to reach Jesus. She reached Jesus, and see what happened."

As Pastor Tim Burgess spoke, Devin squirmed on the padded chair in the youth room. Some of the kids in the room still giggled over the poor woman who appeared earlier in the story, the one who had been bleeding for twelve years. After all, they knew how women bled, what that really meant. He lifted the Bible in his hands and reread the passage about Jesus taking that girl by the hand.

"Hey Tim, are you telling me that if I run out in front of a bus, and I believe hard enough, Jesus will save me from being crushed?" A thick, heavy-boned jokester named Carl asked the question and got a courtesy laugh from his posse, a pair of twin boys that sat on either side of him.

"Not that simple Carl, and none of us could really believe that in our heart. Let me ask you all this. Are any of the people from the Bible still alive and walking the earth today? That means the girl died at some point later on, didn't she? So what point did Christ make by saving her life when he knew she would die later anyway and he knew she was going to a good place if she died right then?"

The room fell quiet for once and Burgess looked glad for it. Devin wondered how Pastor Burgess could stand to try to teach them, having kids screw around with these words like they were in public school. Devin bored in on Burgess, unblinking. *Give me all the answers, send them through my eyes. I need to know now. When I walk out the door, you can't follow me. As much as these churches think they can, they don't go where I've been. I've come to you. You'll never come to me.* Burgess looked at him, but couldn't hold eye contact. *Please, tell me something.*

Devin recognized Burgess' discomfort. The man's fingers began to drum on the armrests of his chair. After no one answered his question, Burgess sighed, built a smile, and settled for a moment on Devin before scanning the rest. "He needed to show that powerful faith would be rewarded in some way, even if our rewards may not be dramatic at first glance. Maybe he needed the people there to be his followers, to touch others. Imagine a family in that room mourning a daughter, a niece, a sister. Dead and gone. And she stands up. Do you think the people in that room became followers? Do you think he got their attention?

"But I think he raised the girl up for a purpose. I have this idea that the girl went on to a life that made quite a difference. Who knows in what way? Jesus decided she needed to be alive. She must have gone on to an incredible life.

"All those things came together. Maybe when someone's life is spared it is a crossroads, a place where roads come in, and where roads radiate out."

When the meeting ended and all the youth moved to the door, Devin remained seated. A cute girl with brown curly hair veered toward Devin and moved her fingertips lightly across his forearm as she walked past. He startled and tensed and seemed to pull right up off the seat. As he looked at her for a moment, he saw her eyes widen, her coy smile disappear, and she swallowed. She broke from his gaze and bolted out the door.

Devin tried to settle his breathing for a bit and cleared his throat.

Burgess shuffled his papers into a folder, and had to sigh again before looking up. "Mr. Thomsen! You are the hungriest listener, which makes me wonder if I am up to the task."

"What task?"

"Answering the questions that shine out of your eyes like a couple of lasers."

"Do you think that God plans in advance when he saves someone from dying or do you think he decides at that instant?"

Burgess nodded, another sigh. "I guess I couldn't know that, Devin. My gut kind of tells me he knows what's coming and has a plan."

"Well, then what does all the praying for the person to be saved do, if it has already been decided in advance?"

"It shows the faith of the person praying."

"But it doesn't actually do anything different for the other person, the dying one?"

"Devin that is an extraordinarily difficult question for me. That kind of thing has been asked for thousands of years. Would you think less of me if I told you I don't know the answer, even if you see it as my job to know?"

"No sir, not at all. But it would be nice if someone did know."

"Yes it would."

When Devin stepped out of the youth room into the hall, Carl and his twin lackeys blocked his way. Carl glanced at his flanking friends and smiled before speaking.

"So, Albino, where was it you said you went to school?"

"Braxton."

"That school is lame. What do you do there, chess?"

"I wrestle."

Carl laughed and put his hands on his hips. He liked to stand too close to people. "That's not a sport! That's a bunch of freaks, grabbing other guys!"

Though Carl was nearly thirty pounds heavier, there was no delay. Devin's headlock came together smoothly. When the larger kid hit the hard hallway floor, the THUD, timed with the grunt of all his air leaving his body at once, drove the twins to opposite walls. Devin walked between them and outside without looking back. Carl wouldn't get up from the floor until he was long gone.

13

As he walked down the hall, Cardsen looked far ahead. Ignoring the sights closer in, he bumped into three kids. Cardsen couldn't take his eyes off Steven at the far end of the hall, talking to Jensen. *That damned Jensen, and Steven is not just saying hi. Great. That's all we need.*

Jensen had all the potential in the world, a likeable and funny smooth talker with devious smarts. The kid also had money and dressed like it, everything fashionable. Hell, even Cardsen liked him. He'd reached out to Jensen last year. They'd shared some humor at football before the kid quit. Sometimes they still traded mild barbs in the hall, despite their split. Liselle Wilkins was trying her angle on him this year, lots of love. Word was out, the lad was the source for anything anyone wanted. A single, rich, traveling dad presented no obstacle to parties at the house. Already Jensen had the administration sifting rumors, counselors sorting tales, and cops beginning to sniff around, and still not Christmas yet. Cardsen knew that the Matchiks and Jensen had grown up together in the same neighborhood. *They keep talking, not good, not good.*

Cardsen finally let the scene go when it came time to turn down the hall where the English classes were taught. He had something else unpleasant to attend to.

"Well well, if it isn't The Coach, down to get kids eligible, make some more excuses for his slugs."

Next Christmas party, I'm punching Louise McCall. I know how to make it look like an accident. I'll tell an animated story near her, throw my arms up, and take out her front teeth with an elbow. But not now, the incompetent wretch has got me kissing her tail.

"Hello to you, too, Louise. Hey, you've got some grading done. The stack's down to nine inches. When you take in that sixth assignment for the quarter, things will get rough again." He moved his head sideways and made a clicking sound in his mouth. Her face darkened. They both knew she found at least five ungraded papers in her stack that had been entered as zeros for the kids. "Did Devin turn in the stuff?"

"He did. His paper on his mom was actually quite good. Too good. He must have been reading Ann Landers last Mother's Day or something. All typed, but lousy spelling and punctuation. And he finished the worksheets. I gave him half on all that, and the paper this week got him his precious D."

"Louise, I want you to know I appreciate this."

"You might, but does he? That kid is the biggest slug I've ever had. He sits and stares at me and shakes. Sharpens his pencil ten times a period, never writes with it. Plays with his fingers. Smirks and giggles at any smart aleck comment. The girls look at him all the time because he's cute I guess. What a mess though, like he sleeps outside every night."

"He's been through some tough stuff, Louise."

McCall glared at him. "Who hasn't? Maybe what he needs is to lose what means the most to him. You being here tells me that is wrestling. Maybe that will get his attention, allow him to rise up above whatever happened."

"I don't know. Seems to me that it's better for him to stay in what gives him confidence."

"To me, it doesn't appear he is gaining much. Sean, you're not doing this little slacker any favors. He needs to bottom out. He won't do anything for himself, and he won't do anything for others unless he's forced."

14

"What's up, Jensen?" Steven stopped at Jensen's locker when the boy made eye contact and acknowledged him with a head bob.

"A lot, Steven. You should come over this weekend. It's been a balls-out party all fall, and you're never there."

"I'm busy, you know."

"Just doing your jock thing. You and your schoolboy friends, you got no idea what you're missing."

"Yeah? Well maybe you should hang with us. Could have used you in football this year."

"Football? Think Cardsen wants me around? I'd have knocked all your dicks in the dirt. You'd have been winners if I was there."

"We won our share."

"You're a sourpuss, Matchik. You never smile anymore. It's been so much better since I gave up all my dad's sports fantasies for me. You should think about that. And you are a regular puss, too. Ellen Michaels. Yeah, you've seen her ass. Last weekend. What do you think about that? She's no vegetarian, that's for sure. I found out first hand."

"Is that right?"

"That's right. And she's got friends. Bunch of rabbits, and all good looking. It's all smooth, Steven, we fly all weekend."

"What does your dad say about all that?"

"Are you serious? What can he say? Man, we're not in second grade anymore, we're in eighth."

Steven began to fidget and turn away, but he stopped himself and looked back at Jensen. "Maybe after wrestling."

"I'm counting on it, Steven."

71

Steven spun around and walked off, leaving Jensen behind. He thought about Ellen Michaels, rolled her over and over in his mind in various conditions and scenarios. Katie Gutierrez kept coming into his head, confusing the picture. He could almost feel Katie's hands on his shoulders after his last match.

"You look uptight, you should be happier after a match like that." She had said. "Do you want a backrub?"

He shrugged and sat in the front row of chairs to watch Overman start his match. Her fingers dug in to his bare shoulders and a peculiar warmth came into his muscles. He had a hard time focusing on Overman's efforts the way he normally did. Overman was growing on him. One thing for sure, the kid was tough, and always fun to watch. But Katie's hands made it so he couldn't even remember if Overman had won.

"Hi Steven."

She gave him a start. How did she materialize in front of him?

"Sorry, you look lost in thought. I didn't mean to startle you."

"Uh, no. I'm not lost. Not lost in thought."

They stood together by some unused lockers as kids emptied the halls in anticipation of the coming bell. Katie looked around and her smile evaporated.

"Steven, here's my phone number. Just in case, you know, if you ever wanted to call." She held out a folded piece of paper.

Steven grabbed at it, more awkward than his coordination typically allowed. He looked from side to side, shoved the paper in the front pocket of his jeans, and walked away from her without a word.

15

"Sean, have you met Karen Matchik?"

Evelyn Cummings gestured with an open hand at the woman who stood as he entered. Cardsen worked his way around the teachers sitting at the counseling conference table and reached out to shake her hand.

"Yes, we met several times last year. Thanks for coming."

"Oh we've met, Mr. Cardsen. And that's not all. I've heard the boys talk about you. You are the one they listen to. Not me, I'm just a mom, they have a great love for you, Mr. Cardsen."

She finished with a smile that one would use for an inside joke. Confused for a moment as to whether he should agree or deny, Cardsen just gave a half nod and found a chair. One thing he did know, the small exchange came loaded with admiration, rivalry, appreciation, and jealousy.

Mrs. Matchik sat down, put her elbows on the table and her manicured fingers in a thoughtful steeple. "I've been informed that my son seems withdrawn and disturbed in class and his grades are dropping. I had hoped to keep some of this private but time has come to share what has happened with his father."

At that moment, her face changed slightly, and Cardsen saw through her façade. This was a tired and beaten woman, desperately hanging on to the remnants of the days when she dispensed judgment and gossip on others with complete confidence in her own position. The ironic rise of eyebrows, the calculated small shake of the head, the sighs, this was how she fought for her dignity as she told the tale of her marriage, of her husband leaving her for a man. The account came unvarnished, but only from her perspective. Each time she mentioned Steven her conflict became evident. Cardsen wondered if he was the only one that realized how closely she identified Steven with his father. She spat her son's name with a disgust she battled to conceal, and then was penitent for the crime of her hatred as she appealed for any help they might bring him.

Cardsen survived with a professional face, staring past her at the master schedule chart in the background. Inside, his heart was wrenching. He tried to wrap his mind around what the Matchik boys were swallowing and came up empty. Less than a week until the tournament ended the season, only a few days to bind Steven to something through blood and sweat.

***

At practice, Cardsen watched the Matchiks more than he should and imagined that he could see the weight they carried in their expressions. Cardsen had brought Matt up on the details. A couple of times Matt caught him looking at one of the brothers. He gave his assistant coach a quick shake of the head and moved on. That night he poured his worries and sadness out to Sonia the way he had about Devin. She sighed and hugged him under the covers. There was nothing she could say.

Through it all, the team kept getting better.

As the ninth and final dual match came and went, Steven destroyed all of his opponents. He toyed with them to get a workout until something would set him off, and he would seek the most pain inflicting move available and apply it. Parents from the other schools shouted at him in anger as he walked off the mat.

Cardsen observed that Steven began to accept contact from Katie after his matches. At other times, he stood apart from the team. Head down and muttering with a scowl. This stopped when Cardsen looked at him, but Steven was too slow to change and the coach always caught him.

Alan Matchik moved rapidly to a top level and sat with a Seven and Two record. After every match, Steven would be the first one to meet him at the edge of the mat and hoist his brother into the air. They gave grimaces rather than smiles. They no longer looked for their parents to attend.

Devin Thomson got past a tough kid from Ickes Junior High in overtime and remained undefeated. The school buzzed with students and adults wanting to know about the crazy little long-haired kid who kicked ass. His attractive radiant stare, held abnormally long, and his twitching body giving a vibe of insanity that heightened their interest. To most his speech remained clipped. He stayed after class one day and actually had a whole conversation with Coach Cardsen about the best Lynyrd Skynyrd songs, snowball fights, and pizza toppings.

Ryan Van Gorder, Austin Reichs, and Thomas Manzanares remained undefeated. Alfred Rice had one loss. Every varsity wrestler had a winning record except Eric Lofton who stood at One and Seven.

When Eric won in week five on a closed-eyes sit-out where his opponent rode too high and fell into a cradle, the team went crazy. It was a home match, and the noise elevated to a point where Lofton didn't hear the whistle and had to be stopped by the ref's hands. When they went to the middle and the ref raised his hand, Lofton looked confused. Then he turned to face the mob of leaping and screaming teammates. Cardsen was right there with them arriving just after Gary Overman, who put his face right in close to Lofton's.

"Dude you won, you really did it. That's right, a win. Do you understand what I'm telling you? That's right, you gave it right to him, stuck his own knee in his mouth, that's what I'm talking about. I taught you that, don't you remember when I taught you that?"

16

Devin walked home that night after practice. His mom made sure he had her raincoat in his gym bag. A mile and a half in all and he sank within himself under the raincoat hood. The streetlights hardly pierced the darkness and rain, only contributing a dancing light off the water running down the gutter next to the sidewalk. A different world altogether. It wasn't like this in LaGrande, out on the dry eastern prairie at the base of those sparse Wallowa forests. Braxton was all right. More than all right, it was good. People showed interest in him, he could tell that now. In fact, he liked playing mysterious with the kids. He hadn't been playing at all at first, but now he knew a few people wanted him as a friend and they pursued him when he stayed aloof. The Matchik brothers kept saying he should come over some Saturday night, and he probably would soon. And Cardsen, he'd never known a man like that. Cardsen had kids. That meant that some people had dads like Cardsen. Actually, he'd never known any man very well. Maybe he and Cardsen could be friends throughout their whole lives.

Under his hood he realized that the thing that seemed to live in the pit of his stomach, the thing that groaned sometimes and echoed into his head, was silent. Looking back, he had always known something else lived inside of him. Most of his years it hadn't mattered, he and that thing had an arrangement for living. Then came the shooting last June. Now that terrible inner partner needed a bigger say. Devin considered all of this silly on some level, but laughing at his own ridiculousness didn't make it go away. Devin looked up into the rain and let it wet his face. He closed his eyes and listened inside himself – nothing. He felt tired but strong at the same time. He realized the groan had been beaten down by the intense workout and his growing confidence, and maybe God helping somehow. Blinking away the water, he saw a telephone pole cutting the glow of a streetlamp uphill. *The cross.*

Tonight he would write that paper for English. A good paper about how writing kept Anne Frank alive inside herself. So good that Mrs. McCall would be looking for plagiarism for days.

The hill became steeper and veered west. A few cars made the water at his feet dance with their headlights. To the east, he was pretty sure, lay the neighborhood where the Matchik brothers lived. Big houses. Real big. Several blocks of apartment buildings covered the hilltop. A set of nice old brick ones with fancy windows. Then practical cinderblock buildings with lots of pickup trucks and rusted Japanese cars in the lots. And finally their complex, vertical wood slats painted in the maroon of a stained picnic table. The paint peeled in big strips and left bare wood showing below. He kicked a soggy Hamm's case to the curb as he walked through the parking lot.

"There you are!" His mom met him at the door, surprising him with a huge smile. She pulled off his raincoat and hung it up. He noticed his sisters had bowls of Spaghetti-o's and carrot sticks. Good, that would be just right for his weight. His mom poured him a bowl from the pan on the stove and sat down across from him.

"Devin, could I get you to clean up and put the girls down tonight? Roxanne's not coming over, and the people I work with are gathering at a coworker's new house to have a housewarming party. It's so exciting. I feel like I'm part of a group here now. The people at work have adopted me and I want to give back to them. It's kind of like my team, do you know what I mean?"

Her son listened, never finished lifting the spoon to his mouth. He set it back. She trusted him with his sisters, an honor. He was proud of her for being good on a team, just like him. Roxanne, the ever present sponsor, not coming, thank God. A nice break from her and the endless AA babble. But there was more, and he couldn't stop thinking about it.

A party. She was going to a party. Now was the time to ask about it, if that was such a good idea to go there. Now was the time.

"Yeah. I can do it." He took a bite. Then he made a face at Leza and she laughed. He didn't look at his mom again.

At nine the girls were in bed. He played dolls with them. He played with their toy farm. It felt good to play with them, something Devin hadn't done since wrestling started. He looked at the clock, time remained to write that paper.

Pointless, something tells me that it would be pointless to write the stupid thing.

What is she going to do at the party?

Monday Night Football blared on the television. He'd never understood football. *Write the paper.*

She didn't say when she'd be home.

Shut it off. Write the paper for the team, districts are coming. Call Cardsen. Write it.

This isn't real. Braxton is not real. Cardsen will be gone from my life soon, just like everyone else but mom. Coach has got plenty of other kids, like his own, and the Matchiks, a much better match for him. He can be proud of them. Not me.

He woke up at one o'clock to laughter. They were laughing and couldn't stop. There was a bottle on the counter and the guy had a mustache and some gray in his hair. He said "Hey, pardner…" when Devin walked out of his bedroom and into the kitchen. His mom leaned against the man.

"Devin, go to bed."

She didn't even look sorry about it. When he turned his back, she was giggling again.

For an hour he heard sounds from outside his room and inside his body. His head felt as if it would explode. Finally, he crept out and sat in the dark hall and watched.

He watched the shadows of limbs pawing, listened to the moaning and the couch creaking under the load.

17

With districts on Saturday, running was dropped from practice. Cardsen didn't want that type of pounding on the leg joints. Strength workouts during the week tapered down to maintenance levels. At the end of practice, aerobics became conditioning with wrestlers taking turns leading skills against air to the pumping music of Social Distortion, Cake, and The Red Hot Chili Peppers. Skill work was interrupted less often to correct mistakes. For three weeks now the wrestlers had been encouraged to strengthen their individual styles, to focus on what they did best, and develop strategies to cover their weak points. Live wrestling grew long and intense. Morale and excitement soared to new heights. Now they understood what Cardsen talked about on the steps nine weeks ago, about how close they would be, about how they would feel, about how much they would learn.

Louise McCall came into Cardsen's classroom before school on Thursday. Cardsen heard a noise while getting some equipment out of a cabinet and was surprised when he turned around. He couldn't recall her ever having been in his room before. She sported a Christmas sweater and glasses with a chain around the back of her neck. Cardsen bristled. He liked controlling contacts that involved tension, and she had him off guard. He moved toward her and sat on a lab table.

"Hey, Louise."

She handed him a grade print-out. At a glance he saw Devin Thomsen printed on top.

"Sean, I wanted to tell you personally. Your boy didn't do his paper on Anne Frank. He's used up his late work privileges. He's done."

80

Cardsen looked down at the print-out. He remained speechless for an awkward time, his jaw working on nothing. Of course, his experience didn't allow him surprise that a kid like Devin could skip his work. After all, kids were capable of any possible error and any level of self-destruction. The championship hopes would take a blow. Team cohesion would take a blow. Somehow he would find a way to live with that. But what stunned and choked him was that Devin Thomsen wouldn't be with them. No one would see his pure, inexhaustible energy at work on the mat. No one would hoist the kid in the air.

For two days in a row, Cardsen had looked for his normal contact with Devin as class ended. Each time the kid mixed in with other students in his row and moved toward the door without eye contact. Devin's edge went dull at practice. On Tuesday, for the first time all year, the coaches yelled at him to get it in gear in a live match. Alan Matchik had been taking it to him. Cardsen regretted not moving on his instincts about Devin earlier in the week. There had been so much going on with Steven, with kids in need in his classes, and with three other mini-crises among the wrestlers (the Matchiks and Thomsens weren't his only troubled families). There were tournament-seed meetings and school conferences at night. Sean Cardsen was on adrenaline. Rest could come next week.

Cardsen sensed that Mrs. McCall was still there. "I honestly thought he'd do it."

"You thought. Looking at you, I see how much this means to you. But don't you see, Sean? You're making it about you. He's sat and stared at me all week with a goofy grin. Honestly, it kind of freaks me out. They say sociopaths stare like that. I don't believe he feels half of what you feel. And he's the one it's supposed to be for. If you think you love this kid, like you want to take him home as one of your own children, you love a mirage. There's nothing there. The kid you think you see doesn't exist. He's smugly waiting to see if you'll save him. If you do he'll do it to everyone he can. He'll just be an embarrassing extension of you, not himself. Then next year he'll be gone and you'll still be here, missing part of yourself."

After McCall left, Sean went through the motions of getting ready for the day. He was driving himself crazy with analysis. *What is a rescuer, an enabler? What is a mentor, a coach? Listen to what McCall said, she knows. What is faith and loyalty in someone? What teaches the most? Can they win it without Devin? Should that matter? Listen to what Liselle said –too close. Can I face losing the kid? Would I care if he was some ugly kid who wasn't very good?*

He got his second period going on a project, interacting little with them as his mind continued to circle. Based on teachings from his foggy religious past, Cardsen seemed sure that he should know what God wanted him to do. But he didn't know. When he appealed with an internal prayer he was embarrassed. He settled a bit when done, and then he decided. *To hell with any moral, character, or values issues.*

Now, the teacher was supposed to hold the kid to a high standard, and much later, the kid would return for a tearful thank you for helping him learn the value of following through. They might do it that way in Hollywood. In fact, Cardsen had starred in that movie before. And just last quarter, with nothing left to try, he had mercilessly failed a student under great stress at home. But this was a different movie, the possibility of a lifetime connection the plotline. Their link was tenuous. Devin Thomsen could disappear from their school at any time. Cardsen knew a transient situation when he saw one. If their link was severed right now and Devin disappeared, all he would take with him would be a hazy memory of failure and Devin would not feel the pain of missing a friend and believer. If he left, Cardsen wanted that pain to be inside Devin. Maybe the pain of missing someone who believed in him could cause him to seek out his coach again, from wherever he was.

Cardsen went over and fetched Liselle from her planning period next door, to come over and cover his class. *If only she knew the subject matter.* That gave him a smile. He went to the office and was fortunate to catch his principal at an available time.

***

"I've never asked for anything like this before. Nine years, you know."

"That's right, you haven't. But now you have." The principal, Thelma Richardson, raised an eyebrow and leaned back on her chair.

Cardsen understood her intimation, it only took once to be like the rest of the cheaters in the world. Richardson and Cardsen liked each other, but they seemed to operate on different planets, each in their own business. Cardsen rarely sent kids down, and Richardson rarely interjected into his world. When times got tough for either one, they got the tacit approval of the other. Richardson couldn't help being happy to go one up on Cardsen, should she so decide. But she knew that wouldn't bother Sean Cardsen as much as his having to swallow the bragging he did about academics coming first for his athletes.

"From what I understand, there's no longer a district eligibility policy for junior high, it's up to us what we do in our own school."

"True, but *we* have a policy." She paused, sighed, and let him wriggle.

Cardsen knew what she must be thinking, *Gees Sean, it's just junior high wrestling.*

Her face softened. "I've seen him at the matches. I met his mother the day she brought him here." She leaned forward. "On all that you know Sean, is this tournament what Devin Thomsen needs?"

"Yes."

"Nothing else needs to be said. It's taken care of. Win us a championship for Braxton will you? We've never gotten by Abe Lincoln in that sport."

"We'll see what we can do." The coach rose from his seat and headed for the door.

"Hey Sean." Cardsen stopped to listen. "How high was Louise McCall's paper stack?"

"Ah… well…" For a moment Cardsen relished the opportunity for revenge, but he let it go, and looked down to the floor. "…she did what she could, that stack is pretty small now."

Cardsen took back his class from Liselle, thanking her for covering for him. The second hour kids were in partnerships, one standing on a chair and dropping a tennis ball, the other timing; potential energy converting to kinetic energy, and finding the percent loss to friction. With the students absorbed in the lab, Cardsen called Devin out to the hall with minimum disruption.

The boy didn't look up. For the first time Cardsen realized how tiny Devin was. Devin shriveled in front of him.

"McCall's English."

Devin's hands were in his pockets, his shoulders shimmying back and forth rhythmically. "I'm sorry."

Cardsen could barely hear his voice.

"I believe you could have done it. I believe you could go do it right now if we took the time."

"I know you do."

"But you don't believe?"

"I don't know about belief. I just didn't do it. I don't know why." He looked up at Cardsen for a moment, and then back down.

"You better be ready to wrestle day after tomorrow because barring you robbing a couple of liquor stores and committing mass murder, you are going to be in the lineup. You want to quit but you won't admit it. You're not allowed to quit."

A shiver undulated through the kid, the shimmies stopped and his hands came out of his pockets, fingers extended and twitching.

"I want one thing." Cardsen said. The eyes flashed up at him. "A promise to write that paper by Monday and give it to McCall, grade or no grade. Can you do it?"

"Yes."

"Go finish your lab."

Devin turned without looking up or speaking and went back in. Cardsen put his hand to his forehead and rubbed. Then he spoke to the wall. "You're welcome."

18

The wrestlers' weights looked good before practice and no injuries stood in their way. The rest of the team survived eligibility, although cases other than Devin's had also approached the Do or Die line. Cardsen and Matt joked in the coach's office that their team's collective IQ might not match Alfred Rice's weight. The last night of practice featured only a rapid skill warm-up, one live match, and an active-passive skill series to keep the sweat going. Junior varsity wrestlers were allowed to sit after warm-ups unless called upon to prepare someone.

Cardsen whistled the end of practice and the team tumbled into the middle of the mat, rolling over each other like bear cubs. Wrestlers lose inhibitions about physical contact and they piled in tight. Overman was on Rice's back like a parasite, jabbering about what he planned to do to his first opponent in the bracket. Seizing the opportunity in close quarters, Austin Reichs shoved Overman so hard that he left Alfred's back and did two log rolls. Steven pulled Devin, who of all the wrestlers wasn't smiling, down beside him. He put his arm around the blonde's shoulders.

"Thomsen, you can win it tomorrow. You can do it."

Devin looked at him and nodded, and then he smiled and answered. "Show me the way."

"So Coach." Alfred Rice stood up, towering over the other kids down on the mat. "Don't try talkin' none until you come through on some music."

"What do you mean, Rice?"

"Aw, don't play dumb with me Coach, we all know what you said to our little man Lofton at the beginning of all this about that Hoe Down. Get us some or we gang up and tear you apart."

Cardsen smiled like a Cheshire cat and he looked to Waters for back up, but the other coach just shrugged.

"I'm with them. Don't expect me to support you."

Cardsen scanned for Lofton, who he found smiling as well. They had already organized themselves before practice. Time to release the pressure; send them out on a light note. No Knute Rockne speeches. All the preparation was done. Nothing left to do but show up and get after it.

"All right, Eric, we better do it." Cardsen fetched his guitar and Lofton's violin from his convenient hiding place in the janitorial closet nearby. They set up and took off on the hillbilly-inspired song. Cardsen struggled with the strings under his hands. He'd practiced at home all season but was tired from the long week. Lofton carried it off with a clean, clear sound on his violin, confident and smiling close-mouthed. During the second verse Overman leapt up, grinning with his braces, and dancing such a ridiculous jig that Rice collapsed back to the mat and Steven Matchik and Devin Thomsen fell to their sides laughing. Katie came in from the side and pulled Coach Waters to his feet. They had time for just a short bit of Cotton-Eyed-Joe before it was all over and Cardsen high-fived Eric Lofton.

"That –was the worst stuff I've ever seen. Don't tell my family or my friends I watched that. Lord get me outta here." But Alfred was all smiles when he said it, and then Ryan Van Gorder started a team dog-pile on him for his insolence until Cardsen broke them up and told them to roll up the mats.

As the coach took his guitar to its case, he saw Liselle Wilkins peering out from behind a pillar at the far side. She had a look somewhere between concern and bewilderment. *Damn, always, every time.* Thought Cardsen. A second later she realized she had been spotted and her body snapped stiff with surprise. She feigned interest in finding a place to throw away her Diet Pepsi can and moved down the hall.

The coach was on his knees snapping up his guitar case when he realized that a kid was standing next to him. He looked up and saw Alan Matchik. Alan had brown hair, straighter than Steven's. He stood shorter than his brother, but wider in the shoulders. His face was ordinary but as American as they come. He could be Jerry Mathers, Tom Sawyer, or a Norman Rockwell face for a Boy-Scout uniform.

"Hey, Coach."

"Hey, Alan."

"I'm going to lead this team next year."

"Yes, I know. We couldn't do better." Cardsen reached up and shook his hand.

***

"Nice dance." Steven caught up to Katie. She turned to smile at him.

"Thanks. My dad is into that country stuff. We all dance at the house sometimes. He wants more Tex-Mex here. You oughta see him around that."

"What's Tex-Mex?"

"Oh, I don't know if I can explain. I've never been to Tex or Mex myself. Your folks, what are they in to?"

Steven felt blood rush to his cheeks. He feared his face would go as dark as the blackness of his hair.

"I don't know. Money I guess. Themselves, maybe." He tried to laugh it off, but couldn't do it right, so he just said "later" and ran ahead to the locker room door. Right before going in, he took one quick look back at her. He remembered the feel of her hands massaging his shoulders when they were tight with anger. She looked sad, like she was slumping down. Steven looked away, turned the knob, and went in.

***

That night, Cardsen played Candyland with his kids, and then shared two glasses of wine with Sonia after the kids went to bed. He told her of the previous day's decision regarding Devin and the antics at their last practice. He talked of several of the other boys, as well as Katie Gutierrez, about how much he'd miss them after wrestling, about how glad he was to have Alan Matchik coming back, and to have Steven in class to keep those ties alive.

When his ramblings slowed, Sonia snuggled tighter on the couch. "Sean, when you risk your reputation for a kid, or risk getting hurt by them, you make me proud to be with you."

"I'm not trying to be a hero. I'm trying to make the right decision. I may sound melodramatic, but sometimes I get the feeling that if I don't make the right decision it could be life or death. Crazy isn't it? Just a little nine week sport."

"You have a gift. You believe in those that can't be believed in. You can carry the weight of whatever happens. I know that. How can anyone know what a good decision is? We never get to see the result of a different choice. You must remember, always remember, that outcomes depend far more on what *they* do, rather than on what *you* do."

***

At that same time, Steven sat at the top of the staircase at his home. All the lights were off. His mom gone to meet the friends who propped her up. The house so quiet that he could hear the echoes of Christmases that had gone before and the boom of his dad's voice and the dart gun fights over the furniture with Alan.

***

Devin reclined on his bed with Kimmy and Leza and a couple of their stuffed animals. They pulled the TV into the bedroom to watch "Lion King" on VCR. He left the door open a crack so he could catch pieces of Roxanne, the bulldog AA sponsor, battling it out with his mother as they debriefed the long week. His inside howled like a storm. His arms, legs, torso, and neck jerked and flexed, disturbing his sisters as he banged against the wall behind his mattress.

19

Every year, at least one kid would freak from the perceived pressure and try to back out of the tournament during the last week of preparation. As Cardsen drove in to Braxton, he considered that he'd seen no obvious signs of disappearing acts or psychosomatic illness. But anything was possible at this age and in this sport. He knew that Alan Matchik would be the highest risk of backing out, although all signs seemed to indicate that he wanted success at this point. Steven clearly wanted a repeat championship and he would drag Alan if need be. Devin Thomsen was a different case. No one, probably not even the kid himself, knew how he'd respond to Cardsen's heavy helping hand. In the lives of the Devin Thomsens of the world, how could one anticipate all hindrances to their presence, especially when due to arrive at six o'clock on a Saturday morning?

It was pitch dark at the school, and Cardsen fumbled twice on his security code to get in only to find Matt already inside, door propped open to the coaches' office. Cardsen entered and set down his coffee. Rather than meeting at the site of the tournament like some of the other teams, they had their wrestlers report to school an hour before weigh-ins, followed by parent car-pools to the site. This routine allowed the coaches a window of time to call late sleepers from their phone list. Also, they could check weights in case someone had to sweat off a pound or two, now illegal in the presence of an official. However such antics were a rare requirement for Braxton on tournament morning, with Cardsen a stickler for squaring it away the day before.

"Is anyone coming today, Matt, or is it only us?"

Matt smiled. "Relax, Sean, they'll be here. Today's the day."

"Today's the day and I'm getting my annual cold."

"Yeah, me too. I'll be barely hanging on during finals today. Man, I like our seeds. We got a good shot. Really good."

"No doubt, if everyone shows. Going undefeated in duals gives me a funny feeling, like we're primed for knockoffs."

"You're paranoid Sean. This is a good team and they're all coming."

They all came. Devin arrived five minutes after six and responded with a polite nod to the 'good mornings' and giddy grins from his coaches. The Matchik brothers arrived together, surprisingly awake. Weights went well except for Overman. Typically three pounds under his weight class, he was right at his limit, with the potential for scale variation at the tournament a problem. If someone does not make weight they are out of the tournament on the spot.

"Overman, what did you eat? You're five pounds heavier than last night!"

"Oh, Coach, just had some energy food. Like for a long day. Thought of it like I was climbing Hood, you know how you're supposed to do that? Build up the carbs. So I ate a big bag of trail mix and three bowls of cereal, and I guess after that I had dinner and a whole bunch of popcorn. Played my dad in Madden Football, vid game you know? You play that, Coach? Wow. Guess I ate a lot. Guess I'm right on weight."

Cardsen shook his head, in awe of Gary Overman's ignorance of everything they had talked about. He tried to gather himself to cut in but wound up waiting for Overman to take a breath. "Can you take a crap before we go over there?"

"Yeah. I think I got a huge python living up inside of me, time to set it free. You want me to show it to…"

"Overman, you're on your own. Try to do it and don't talk to me anymore. If you do, I'll throw myself under your family van out there."

The tournament was at Darby High School, six miles to the southwest, by the Clackamas River. The rain had stopped but the roads were still wet, and at that early hour the sun couldn't do much to the overcast sky but change it from black to dark grey. The coaches rode together in Cardsen's GMC and the kids split among the five volunteer parents. On arrival, Braxton set up a home base in a lower corner of the stands in time to be called to weigh-ins. Cardsen found great relief when there were no problems. After he weighed in, Overman came near and whispered.

"You should have seen it, Coach."

Cardsen cringed, pretending not to hear.

The first round loomed minutes away and the wrestlers from all the schools were hyper. Teammates tumbled over each other, chased and tackled each other. All nine teams had brightly colored sweats, and the burnt orange of Braxton took a corner of the three-mat area to start warming up. The coaches left Ryan Van Gorder to lead the team while they relaxed in the stands, looking uninterested but actually studying their own kids and the other teams. All of the Braxton kids appeared so alive, quick, and smooth as they did their skills. Cardsen was very proud to see them. He had a good feeling, but anything could happen at a tournament.

One thing concerned him. Devin Thomsen's motor. Through the season, Cardsen began to realize that he had never seen a kid with that level of physical energy. Devin's patented bouncing and constant movement of every possible muscle, his sawing through kids before a match, had initially spurred Cardsen to try and rein him in. But Cardsen came to realize that the kid always retained enough energy to wrestle, and the remarkable metabolism was key to who he was. Now, while Devin's skills looked smooth, his body remained still in-between actions. His face showed lethargy, a look no one had seen before.

Elia Azan, their little 75 pounder, got Braxton off to a great start. Eric Lofton wrestled the top seed and hustled until he was pinned early in the second period. Devin hardly moved as he warmed up, but Cardsen had no time to go try and light a fire under him. The coach knew he'd played most of his hand with Devin. The kid had come. He brought his messed up little self to be with the team. Cardsen would never forget that. No matter what happened today, he'd never let Devin's contributions to the team be erased. The time had come to let him go and focus on the other kids.

As Cardsen accompanied Devin to his first match, he could overhear the Foster team talking about Devin. *Yeah, that kid, he's really tough, I heard he is undefeated. Yeah he is weird looking. I heard that's because he's from some other country and he was the champion over there.*

The wrestler from Foster wasn't the low seed because of losses, he had been injured most of the season and hadn't collected bracketing points. His skills were well above average. Still, it was agony for Waters and Cardsen to watch him outwit Devin Thomsen at every turn. Devin stood dead on his feet, no flashing double-leg or fireman's carry. The Foster kid turned a sloppy shot by Devin into a two point near-fall and went up 4-0. Devin showed a burst and quickly reversed, powering his opponent to his back. For a moment it looked like old times but there was a confused looked on Devin's face and he had no power to put the match away. His opponent fought out and achieved his own reversal. From there to the end of the match it was Devin showing a feeble effort on bottom and a strong but inexperienced wrestler riding him tough. The kids from Foster

Middle went crazy with the upset of the number-one-seed from Braxton.

***

An out-of-focus bad dream. The gym lights, the echoes and the humming noises. The end of the season was coming today and what was he beyond the season? Devin's mouth was dry. He couldn't sweat. The groan inside him died out in the middle of the night. He woke up empty, terrifyingly empty. No fear, no excitement, no concerns about the day. Then, as his mom drove him to Braxton, a new feeling came and grew stronger. This whole season had been a sham, a joke. He was their mascot, not their champion. By the time he arrived, he was convinced that the team had spent the season laughing at him behind his back.

How could they not? Small, weak, stupid, white like snow, poor, uncool. If the guys saw how he lived, how he had always lived, they would laugh at him so hard. His mom, what would they say if they knew her? They'd laugh. If they saw me on my knees, at the mercy of some stinky freak, they'd laugh about that too. And now out on the mat, I've given nothing. They'll be laughing now for sure. That's it, that's the whistle. Where is the scoreboard? 10 to 7. I didn't score ten, that's for sure.

***

Cardsen gripped Matt Waters' tricep as Devin's match came to a close. He spoke loudly into his ear over the cheering fans. "Keep him close. Make sure he stays with the team. Nothing negative. After you talk to him, ask Alfred Rice to sit with him a while. I'll get with him when I can. We'll need whatever we can get out of him."

Cardsen wanted to stay and let Devin know he was still on his side, that they had a long day ahead. But Cardsen needed to hustle over and give Alan Matchik a last build-up for his match.

It was imperative that Alan get a win so that the losses by Lofton and Thomsen didn't start a negative roll. When he arrived at Alan's mat, Steven stood there with his brother, wide-eyed, swinging his arms.

"Thomsen lost? How did he lose? How could he lose? He had to have quit, why did he quit?"

"Steven, close your mouth, he didn't quit. Things happen at District. What's important is Alan. We'll get Thomsen back. You'll see." Irritation at Steven's comments and negative energy right before his brother's match could be heard in Cardsen's voice. And the fear that what happened to Devin could somehow happen to Steven as well, on the same day.

Alan was magnificent. He wrestled as if he had been doing it for five years. Poise, confidence, and intelligence showed in all he did. His opponent came out overly aggressive and Alan scored a takedown on a shuck. Then cradle after cradle, just unable to get the near shoulder down for a pin. Finally, with under a minute left in the match and Alan threatening to score a technical fall due to the high score, Cardsen encouraged him to try another finish and get the pin. Each pin won an extra point in the tournament, and they'd need all they could get to stay with Abe Lincoln.

When Alan came off the mat the entire Braxton team, sans Devin, met him one by one. The electricity was back. From that moment on, with or without Devin Thomsen, Braxton would make a run.

What a run it was. Twelve wins in a row to finish the round. By the time Austin Reichs overpowered a stout kid from Abe Lincoln in 45 seconds at 167 pounds, everyone knew Lincoln was in trouble.

Despite a 46-36 loss to Braxton in their dual match, Lincoln's coach had expressed his confidence at the morning coach's meeting that it would be Lincoln's day once again.

They would turn the upstarts to also-rans at the tournament. "Cardsen," he said, "you've done a great job but your kids are too quirky. You're on a razor's edge. Good luck holding on."

"We'll see what you think at four o'clock this afternoon," said Cardsen, not at all pleased by the condescension.

Steven appeared to be untouchable. Any worries his coaches had about him evaporated in the first seconds of his match. Physically, he was much more powerful and athletic than the other kids his size and his skills were equally a cut above. Steven didn't indulge his desire for violence in the first match. His overmatched opponent succumbed to a pin and the match ended almost before it began. To Cardsen, Steven looked disappointed and Cardsen could sense the desire to kill coming off of his wrestler. The kid wanted to inflict pain, and he wanted his opponents to stand up to him so he would have a good excuse.

Cardsen was elated. Twice in his tenure Braxton had taken third place. Once they had taken second place. But those teams never threatened the champions, Abe Lincoln, who won by large margins each time.

Cardsen never did get time to join Devin and debrief the match, but every few minutes Cardsen looked into the stands to check on him. When the first round ended they would have to talk. Cardsen would remind Devin of the need to wrestle back for third place, to move forward. Devin stayed by himself for a few matches, but did not disappear. Katie sat with him for a while. By the time Ryan Van Gorder won at 126 pounds, Devin joined the team to congratulate the winners coming off. Cardsen found a chance to reach over and give Devin's shoulder a reassuring squeeze.

***

Katie sat down gently next to Devin Thomsen. His chest heaved, more from shock than exhaustion. His singlet straps were down to reveal his upper body, and his hair was wild all over. He hadn't talked to her much during the season. She seemed so unapproachable, so straight and dignified, and he just some wild animal. Yet here she was. What could he say to her? When he looked at her she seemed to freeze for a moment, like she was stunned by his gaze. He didn't say anything to her, just stared and kept breathing, chest heaving along with his unwelcome partner inside.

"Hey." She smiled

He said nothing in return.

"Hey, Devin, how are you? Are you all right?"

"Yeah, I'm fine." He broke his stare and looked down at his feet.

"Do you know something? The guys talk about you some."

He twitched, his left hand came up to his temple and stroked the side of his head. Stroked his scar. "Yeah, I imagine they do."

"They say that this season could have never happened if you hadn't come here. Steven was telling Ryan that he tries to move like you do. And then Ryan said you shine light out, like some angel they study at their church."

Devin looked at her again. "I let everybody down. You have no idea how much."

"How is it letting everybody down when you made them what they are?" Katie fidgeted under his gaze as she waited for him to answer but he only stared. She sighed and seemed to calm without breaking eye contact.

"Hey Devin, you wrestle again after lunch, right? I'm going to sit right by the mat for that match, because I know it's going to be a lot different from this morning."

***

The tournament continued immediately into the semifinals. Of the fourteen that wrestled, Braxton won eight, which included both Matchik brothers and Ryan Van Gorder. They were sending eight out of sixteen weights to the finals. Abe Lincoln was sending six, and Braxton had built a fairly strong lead. The other seven teams had the remainder of the final slots about evenly divided and there would be no other contenders for the team title.

The noise in the gym built steadily to a constant roar. Each individual match brought mobs of screaming fans. Any conversation had to be done at a shout, and on the floor, coaches were losing their voices one by one.

Steven's semifinal was a rematch with the kid from Sunnyside. The Sunnyside wrestler's strategy was to use his strength to turn the match into a low-skill slugfest. He forced his way into a head-tie after the whistle and when Steven moved in for a set-up, the kid flung him toward the boundary line where Steven did a seat roll and came back to his feet. The noise level soared in the Sunnyside crowd. The move looked tough and macho, but meant nothing in the context of wrestling. The referee moved them back to the middle and the Sunnyside wrestler tried an intimidating glare. At the whistle he slapped Steven in the face, jabbed at his nose, and reached again for the head-tie.

Steven dropped and took a single-leg, wrapping it tight and taking the leg very high. He kept the other boy hopping on one leg longer than needed until some laughs from wrestlers watching could be heard. Then he levered him into the air using the leg and put his opponent down as hard as he could get away with. From there he moved to control position and broke the kid down to his belly.

Steven's eyes watered from his nose having been jabbed straight in. His insides were in a fury but instead of emoting, he acted like a cold technician in the lethal injection chamber. He worked his way to a tight chicken-wing on one arm and took his time to get the other arm in a chicken-wing. When that rare move was achieved, the crowd, pro and con, let out their breath because in a junior high match that meant the end would be soon. Steven took his time. He could hear the desperation in the noises his opponent was making, including some quiet swearing. He continued to tighten the move and heard the pitch of the sounds rise with his opponent's pain. Steven ran the finish to the move part way and tightened some more. Then he sat through and stayed there, intentionally not flattening the shoulders of the other wrestler. The kid was in agony. He was under such stress that his voice issued only inhuman sounds. In a double-chicken-wing, the more muscular the kid held in the hold, the more pain he feels when his big arms are pulled impossibly far back. The referee looked concerned but despite the stress didn't see the move to be potentially dangerous for serious injury and didn't intervene. Steven could see the clock from their location on the mat and he waited for the twenty-second mark, even though Cardsen had been yelling at him thirty seconds earlier to finish it. Finally, he moved the kid's back enough to get the pin. Steven regretted that he couldn't look into the kid's eyes at the moment when it would be all over. He regretted that there would be no blood.

His opponent couldn't rise off of the mat for some time and Steven didn't try to help, he just waited at the mark. His opponent's mother was at mat level screaming.

"You little bastard, you suck! Disqualify him! That's bullshit! Throw him out!"

The tournament director, along with a policeman working security, guided her away as she continued to scream over their shoulders.

***

As everyone moved back to the stands, Cardsen's old friend, the Sunnyside coach, wound up near him shaking his head, not sure how mad to be. He put his head close to Cardsen's to avoid shouting.

"That *was* chickenshit Sean."

"No, it's called a chicken-wing. And that kid's mom, are you saying she is Mother Theresa? And that nose poke, you guys been working on that? Are you teaching that as an effective wrestling move now?" By the time he finished, they were both smiling and nearly laughing.

Catching up to Steven near the door out of the gym, Cardsen cut him off by stepping in front of him. With him the coach was curt and unforgiving. "Are you interested in listening to coaching? Or do you have your own plan for today?"

For just an instant Steven responded to the challenge with a nasty expression, but he let it fade as he looked into Cardsen's face and he looked down at his toes. "You're the coach."

"I'm interested in you being a champion. Are you more interested in being a champion or being a thug?"

"I want to repeat as champion."

"Do you think you'll put that Lincoln kid in a double-chicken-wing in the finals? If you're thinking more about hurting him than winning he's going to give you a surprise. Because he's good enough to take care of a thug the way we try. Thugs get shown for what they are in the end. Personally, I enjoyed you taking that kid apart just now until the crap at the end. If I'm telling you to end it and you ignore me, in my book that's an F-you."

Steven didn't look up. "That's not what I intended. You coach everyone to be rough. I want to be rough."

"I coach that way because I have a bunch of soft suburban flesh that's been taught to fear pain. You've mastered that already and we both know it. Don't use my words against me because you know I try for a little sportsmanship as well."

He looked up and sought eye contact. Cardsen saw sincerity in his face but in the eyes, darkness, sadness, fear. And he saw tears.

"I'm sorry, Coach. Tell me what I need to do. Don't let me screw it up."

"Accepted. What to do? Try committing to going just as hard, but focus on yourself, not your opponent. You have superior skills so don't let them pull you into their style. Try enjoying winning a little bit. And for once, enjoy being so damned gifted."

***

When the semifinals came to an end an hour later, Cardsen cautioned his kids about what to eat for lunch and set a deadline for return. He cornered Ryan Van Gorder and without humility demanded that Ryan accompany Devin to lunch and buy him lunch if the kid had no money. Across the street from the school there was a shopping mall with a large food court and they did a huge business on tournament day.

20

The first wrestle-back match arrived for Devin just after lunch. Katie came as close to the mat as rules allowed and Devin noticed her there before the match started. His body began to feel a return to its natural urge for constant movement but warm-up time was very short. Steven came to urge him on. His mother and sisters also arrived, and he saw his sisters take off with a little boy and girl to run to the top of the stands to play.

Can't blame 'em, it looks like fun. Devin looked away from the stands. Time to roll.

Slicing in to earn a quick takedown, Devin realized that while he may be ready to compete again he would not be able to get back to top form. Too much had been taken out of him, or let go by him, he was unsure which. He willed himself to imitate his image as best he could and dispatched his opponent by the second period. Every teammate waited for him when he came off, including JV teammates in street clothes. Every one of them put a hand to him as he walked though their crowd.

Less than an hour later he was warming up again. A win would put him in the match for third place. He recognized the children his sisters were playing with as Cardsen's kids. A quick fantasy of their families joined somehow. He did everything he could to get going. He ran up stairs, jump-roped, bounced and did skills. He rubbed his eyes and slapped himself all over. But his body had always led him, not the other way around. And it was done for the season. His mind became frenetic, fear his new emotion. He did not fear losing. He feared his new diminished energy could be permanent.

The last two months were replaying over and over in his mind. He saw himself running in the halls. No one could stay with him for all of the sprints. No one could last through all the spin drills like him. Being completely physically alive, hearing every muscle in his body –that made him who he was.

God, don't take it from me. He wondered if that could be called a prayer.

It was a close match with questionable calls, leaving Cardsen mad. But in the end the other kid had wrestled an inspired match and Devin Thomsen was out of the tournament. Cardsen reached out to put an arm around him after the match but Devin dodged the gesture, and went into the stands to sit next to his mom. He stayed for an hour, without talking, then rejoined his team.

***

Eight wrestlers in the finals yielded six champions; Steven Matchik, Ryan Van Gorder, Thomas Manzanares, Austin Reichs, Gary Overman, and Alfred Rice.

Alan Matchik was no match for his opponent in the finals and fell by a 10-0 score. He nearly lost on the five-minute blood-time limit as both nostrils poured out from the pounding he took. As Alan came off, one eye swelling toward shut, trying to decide if he should cry, Cardsen gave only smiles and demanded he hold his head high, reminding him of what a run he had made.

Alan climbed the awards stand to the second place position, gauze still stuffed in both nostrils. Camera flashes went off and he did a double take. One of those taking pictures was his mother. They tried for a half-hearted hug afterward. She touched his swollen eyebrow.

"God, I hate this sport, but I do love you, Alan."

As Alan collected his rewards, Steven warmed up by the edge of the stands. He had seen his mom out in front of the award stand. He knew what she said. She did not look at him. He was both surprised and pleased that it had little effect on him. At that moment, Steven knew that he was going to win. It was all business now, the business of winning. For no one else. For himself. His body demanded focus. It was in charge. He dare not let it down, so his mind looked out of his head as the pilot of a sophisticated fighter jet looks out of the cockpit.

When he climbed to the top spot on the stand for the second time in his Braxton career, Steven waved at Katie who stood nearby. Then he gave his mom the old smile, the one from months ago. He wanted a picture of that smile to look back on.

Tonight things were going to change. When Steven got home, he was calling Jensen, as he said he would when wrestling ended. He would head over there to that house to see what all the stories were about. Find out what things went on there. His body would lead him. From now on, his body would always be listened to, never denied.

***

A few kids from the team returned to Braxton that night to get their things, but now they were long gone. Matt Waters had gone home. Sonia and the kids were waiting at the restaurant for him. The district traveling trophy sat on a desk in the coaches' office. He looked at it again and then shut off the light, stepped into the hall, and closed the door.

He pulled a piece of paper out of his pocket for the third time since the last wrestler left. A raggedly torn corner of notebook paper.

Dear coach cardsun
this was the very best wrestling seson
I've got to have
sincerely,
Devin Thomsen

II

21

June, 2006

Devin Thomsen didn't enjoy smoking tobacco, but he inhaled. After all, the acrid taste inside his mouth gave something, the absence of nothing. Big waves crossed each other straight out from where he sat, a riptide of dirty grey that threw spume in the conflict. A couple in sweatshirts walked by hand-in-hand and gave him a quick look. The man immediately looked away but the woman stared at him. When he made direct eye contact her curiosity was overcome and she turned as well. The stout breeze blew a plastic bag past his line of sight on the wet sand, reflecting diffuse light from the sun, fuzzy behind a cloud. Shirtless, he shivered. It was beautiful.

"What do you think, Cotton?"

Devin shrugged. His hand shook when he pulled the cigarette out of his mouth. "Nice day."

"Yeah. What do you think, you going to try to get a hold of her?"

Devin looked up and over at his self-appointed protector from the home. Glendon something. A shriveled bag of brown skin and whiskers. Exact age indeterminate. Speaking through his own cigarette dangling from the corner of his mouth. Skinny arms stuck out of a black T-shirt with the sleeves cut off at the shoulders. Bird-like legs, a full shade lighter than the rest of him, protruded from cutoffs.

Last night in group Glendon talked about how he once ripped off a loaf of bread and a package of chocolate Snack-pack puddings from the Kum and Go. He made soggy sandwiches at a park to the laughter of people walking by. Somehow that set off a sort of epiphany. Fascinating stuff.

"Maybe. She said she'd get my sisters back if she went down to Medford. She's got her hands full."

Like the woman who walked by, Glendon recoiled from the eye contact and looked down at the sand.

"You might be ready, Cotton. You got more going for you than any of us. A real future. Not one sweeping up and emptying trash. You might be able to do it. 'Course Les would know best."

"Yeah, we talk about it most days." Devin stared out to the waves. He wasn't fond of being called Cotton, but he didn't want the guys to know his real name. For all the support they'd given him, Devin couldn't see wanting them to find him in the future.

The sand was grey-black. He knew his chopped white hair and pink skin would contrast against it. Like cotton. Devin wore only stained green skater jeans and goose-bumps from the wind. He took another drag from his cigarette.

"Kid, you're the one we're going to send back. You don't belong here with us."

"I've done it all wrong, same as you."

"You're a kid. What's my excuse? You know, people like me usually aren't still alive at my age."

"And kids my age usually don't drop this far."

"Right Cotton, so don't stay here with us forever. The guys like you. Maybe too much. I don't know if you've noticed how some of them look at you."

Devin pulled out his cigarette and gave Glendon a bit of a glare. Glendon was right about that, but Glendon probably looked at him that way more than any of the rest of them.

"Sorry, kid. They won't do nothin'. They wouldn't dare, and I'll watch out for you."

"I 'preciate it I guess." Devin twisted his upper body, and saw that some men from their home were playing football on the beach. A couple of others tossed a Frisbee.

"When I see you, Cotton, I know there is a ray of hope in the world. When you go out, you'll be all of us. All of us that are too far gone, too old. I'm not the only one that says that."

Talk was getting a bit heavy on the beach, and they still had group ahead tonight. Devin laughed to lighten things up. "Too much pressure, Glendon. But for you guys, I'll do my best. I promise."

"Hey, Cotton?"

"Yeah."

"You sixteen yet?"

Devin didn't look at Glendon but focused out on the waves. "I think I have been for a while. What's today?"

***

Les was looking down at some papers, bald spot in thin brown hair staring back at Devin as he entered the Head Man's office for their daily four-forty meeting. Les heard the boy enter and flattened his beefy hands on his desk, the backs of which were covered with tattoos. His face came up, a smile breaking his pock-marked face.

"Right on time, Devin. Making my day!"

Devin nodded and tried for a smile but it faded into his little smirk. It sounded good to have someone call him by his name. "Thanks for sticking with our schedule."

"Glad to make the time. For you, I need to make the time. We open our third home, the second men's home, up in Warrenton next week. That means daily runs between Lewiston and there. We're bringing our people home, Devin. We're going to capture some of them back from their bondage. There's so damn many, my friend, so many."

Les came out from behind the desk and sat on a beat-up second-hand kitchen chair opposite Devin, who settled in the threadbare recliner. "You smell like shit. Glendon gave you cigarettes again didn't he? I'm going to climb all over that old man. See to it he gets an extra day of toilets."

Devin showed something a little closer to a smile. "Let him be. I can always say no."

"You can always say no. Listen to you. That's why you live here, right?"

"You know how it is."

Les nodded in appreciation of the acknowledgment that he was still one of them. He nodded and grunted, then leaned forward with an elbow on a knee.

"Kid, I've been thinking. Part of me would feel ok about you leaving under the conditions we discussed. Obviously, you're not a prisoner here, but you said you'd listen to what I thought. Do you remember the things we talked about?"

Devin nodded and counted off by touching his fingers. "Yep. Contact a group. Get a temporary sponsor until I find a good match. Contact my mother to see if she has a group, a sponsor, and a place to live. See about what programs they have at the high school. Be assertive about alternative programs that can catch me up for a diploma. Finish the step I'm on. Thank everyone. Get transport."

"If your mom hasn't made it far enough to live with her?"

"Call Coach Sean Cardsen in Braxton."

"Nice. Now I've been thinking. It's only June. If you'll hear me out, I have this idea that we should add another condition, one which will probably keep you here a while longer in the summer. If you agree to it. It comes from listening to you talk in group, from getting to know you."

"I like it here by the beach, but it gets old living with all these guys. No offense Les."

Les laughed a bit. "No offense taken, but thanks a lot for reminding me how I've chosen to live my life." He leaned forward, now serious. "Here it is. I think you should get yourself in top physical condition before you leave. Everyday after work, get on running and strength. Not just a little shape, wrestling type shape. If you make it to Medford you need to try and wrestle at the high school."

Devin couldn't speak for a nearly a minute. Of course he had thought about high school wrestling, fantasized about being something special in the sport. However, for over a year he had tagged that idea as long gone from reality. Resigned himself to being done. Les squinted at him like a tough guy, challenging him. Through all the drama of the meetings, Devin rarely came close to crying. He told his stories with a cold objectivity. Now he choked up, eyes a little bit wet. He could never let go, never. If he did, it would be a flood that went on forever. "Maybe I could do that."

Les raised an eyebrow when he heard Devin's voice crack with actual emotion. Then he nodded. "You'll have the biggest fan base in all of Oregon."

"Les,"

"Yes?"

"I want to go down in the basement."

Les pulled up, surprised. "You mean now?"

"Yes."

"Just the two of us?"

"Yes sir."

Les nearly leapt out of his chair. Color rushed into his face and he wasted no time.

The basement was an eerie part of the big old house, concrete floor and pipes running openly under the already low ceiling. The heating-oil furnace and ultra-large hot water heater took up one corner. The commercial sized washer and dryer took another corner. It was a damp dungeon of a place with a ragged-cut six-foot by six-foot section of shag carpet in the middle of the floor. Les could barely contain his excitement as he shuffled about the room, gathering a few things. Then he came to face Devin.

"You know, people say I don't have the right to do this at all, let alone the authority to do this with you."

"So I've heard."

"We have to do this down here because my donors would never go for it if they saw a hint of this upstairs. Our only secret here, right?"

"Right."

"This is your choice, right?"

"Please, Les."

"Do you want to get on your knees?"

Without answering, Devin put his knees down on the carpet. Les came nearer, stopping by a small table on the carpet. He lifted his hands and spread them. Devin was trembling and Les' eyes filled with tears as he spoke.

"On the night in which he was betrayed, our Lord Jesus took bread, gave thanks, broke it, and gave it to his disciples, saying, 'Take, eat: this is my body, given for you. Do this in remembrance of me.' Again, after supper, he took the cup, gave thanks, and gave it for all to drink, saying, 'This cup is the new covenant in my blood, shed for you and for all people for the forgiveness of sin. Do this in remembrance of me.'"

22

By early August Devin could run the length of the beach from river to sea wall and back twice, a distance of about five miles. He kept a strong pace in the loose sand and added hundreds of yards of dead sprints on the hard, wet sand. Running was good, very good. His lungs and legs strengthened remarkably. By some miracle his body was not as ruined as he feared. To get where he needed to be he would need to wrestle. No workout could replace the shape and learning a body needed to gain through the actual experience. Les was trying to locate the Lewiston High School coach for him to see if they did anything in the summer that he could beg to join.

The third time he ran past the place Devin realized why the men in period dress stoked the smoky fires under the huge driftwood trunk. They were people from the Fort Clatsop reconstruction reenacting the Lewis and Clark Salt Camp. Plaques in town described what had gone on with that camp. He changed his path and headed toward the site. Tourists gathered around and Devin dodged his way in to get a quick view of the set-up.

A large cauldron boiled. The men used sticks to move smaller boiling buckets to different fires. An older reenactor ordered an enthusiastic teenage boy around. The wind blew the smoke plume toward Devin's face. He stayed a bit longer, legs twitching and angry at the interruption in their workout. Inside him the groaning began. He felt the bottom dropping out. Time to run away from the scene. *Jesus turn me away, help me run.*

Devin glanced back over his shoulder at the cooks in the salt camp as he ran. He pumped his legs more furiously than ever, choosing a pounding heart over its competition inside him. His mind's eye gave him an objective view, like when people die for a bit and then see themselves and everything around them that they shouldn't be able to see. Maybe if he focused and pushed himself hard enough he could stop the flood of memories that were coming.

***

The lab lay fifty feet behind the Nehats North Bait and Boats Shop in an old heated boat shed. Many days Devin went straight from work in the legitimate shop to cooking up crank in the hidden old shed, overgrown with a blackberry bush.

A tiny fan blew the garlicky smell off the boiling liquid toward a half open window. Sometimes the miasma made him stagger out for air, or when he was in a down time from using, to vomit. Later, lying down on his mattress in the garage he could smell the chemicals oozing back out of himself. But by then he didn't care.

The weeks he used, his boss, Arthur Childs, let him smoke some every day, and then he binged through the weekend. Arthur would laugh at him and then dock his pay for the extra he consumed.

Devin shook so much that burning dope would often drop onto the back of a hand. Sometimes he'd just watch it burn into his skin.

Arthur's house was across the street and up the hill from the shop. He inherited the place from his father. Rain-drenched boredom, loneliness, and maybe the smell of the crabs and baitfish, led him to start the endless party. Many mornings Arthur somehow cleared the people from the floors of his house, sent his crabbing guides off with tourist parties, and rented out a boat or two.

Devin, who often hadn't slept, would be loading live bait, checking and fueling boat engines, and picking up the smelly detritus from the crabs and fish cleaned the previous day. He would then scrub boats and walls until they were spotless, in contrast to the unspeakable filth of the clothes he had on. His straight blonde hair was so greasy it appeared to have been spiked to multiple points in some deliberate fashion. His wild eyes darted everywhere, like a bird looking for food.

Arthur never looked him in the eyes, saying they were impossible to look at. He said they seemed to look into his soul, and no one had a right to do that. After he left, Devin could never quite picture Arthur in his head. The man could have been anyone. He never remembered looking him full in his face. Days passed like a flip book. Imagery was constant but so overwhelming that little would be remembered long term. On using days the groan inside of him was satisfied. It didn't stand a chance. Devin raced out ahead of it. Far ahead.

He worked frenetically, running from shed to shed, leaping to some job.

Sometimes if the weather broke and he was ahead on work, he would skateboard to the small fishing town on the state highway. From there he would catch a bus up to Lewiston where he skated like a fiend on the promenade. Even the craziest of the packs of kids there, some who later thought they recognized him when he came to town for rehab, were reluctant to talk to him except to sell him marijuana. When the rain drummed outside and night settled in with nothing to do, Devin would play video games all night as if it were a real war on the machine Arthur set up for him in the garage.

Partying at Arthur's, Devin met Eydie Blyeth. She was older than him, hollow-eyed and thin. He enjoyed touching her brown hair, always clean and in a ponytail. She had a nice smile. He wasn't sure what they talked about but Devin knew he liked her.

Several times he remembered smoking crank with her. She gave him pills to make him last forever. Then he pounded her endlessly, hands gripped on her arms, their skin unnaturally alive, like it was crawling off of each of them, mixing and joining as a single skin. Each of them grinding their teeth, her thrashing under him. Colors filled his eyes. That was what he remembered. He kept going long after it should have ended. What should take minutes turned to hours. Sensations once reserved for the final seconds became endless. Eydie found ways to push away, exhausted. He never realized she was gone, his body still moving.

From how Arthur would laugh and quiz him about it the next day, Devin knew that his boss watched them each time.

One day, Arthur told him her parents came from Portland and took her home and she was gone from him. A couple of times he thought he might try to find her but he couldn't spell her last name, and there was today to take care of.

Crank to cook and fish to clean.

Every six or seven days the crash came. He'd sleep through at least a day and two nights. Sometimes Arthur would leave a door open to the garage and he'd wake up freezing, desperately disoriented, teeth chattering.

His self-loathing was limitless, unbound. He moved through the motions of his job, each waking hour an endless fixation on the crime of his existence.

His memory went back to Braxton where he and Steven decided time had come to go beyond the pot, booze, and coke they learned about at Jensen's. His mom had the savvy of an addict and when it was evident how far he'd gone in his use, it undid her. Five months later he slept on floors of people he didn't know. Social services had his sisters and his mom moved in with a tavern owner in southeast Portland. How quickly he did what Roy and Cracker had never been able to do. The apparent loss of her son took his mother's strength much quicker than the hell of her parade of addicted lovers.

He was worse than them.

Devin knew it. And for that, he never wanted forgiveness. If there was a way God could help him be clean and reconciled with his family, that was a miracle he could accept, he could dream about. But he tempered that dream with the ironclad condition that he never be forgiven for knocking down his mother, taking away her fight.

Coach Cardsen would also appear in his thoughts. He remembered when Coach tracked him down somehow at that place off of 82nd. The tweakers stared at the man like he arrived from another planet. Cardsen walked in, ignored them, and practically begged Devin to come stay with him for a while. Devin would fixate in his memory on that peculiar expression, a mixture of strength and defeat, that Cardsen wore like a mask when Devin said; "I have everything I need right here."

Coach had a lot of time to think about how the little puke, Devin from Hicksville, took down his favorite kids, the Matchik brothers.

What a well-deserved hatred that man must feel for him.

He would assure himself that his use of what he and Steven called the 'real stuff', methamphetamine, was over. (Why couldn't he say that word, methamphetamine, out loud?) After all, when he woke up from a crash it wasn't like he felt like running out and smoking the shit. Surely he could walk away. He just liked the way it made him feel when he really wanted to *feel*, how it ran that bastard down that lived inside of him. Could his mother and Cardsen find a way to understand that the feeling was stronger than their love? He wished they could understand their love was something special, irreplaceable. But late on a rainy night, couldn't they know that the stuff was better, more fulfilling?

Each crash brought him assurance that meth and all that came with it fell to the past. He'd instead smoke some pot out of his bong. It would get him through, lift the depression a bit. Then he'd imagine running again, maybe going to high school. The week would wear on; the low wouldn't lift. It drowned him. And that's when he fixated on the gun in his mouth, wanting the blast inside his mouth where he could taste the powder just as his head exploded behind it. Or a bullet through his left eye, dead on through the eye, slicing him away from all of his brain but sleep.

The pounding and the groaning inside of him grew as the days since his last hits of meth stretched out. Towards the end, his head would be filled with screams, and he would cut himself. Not slicing with sharp knives, but digging at his forearms with rusty nails and screwdrivers, blunt and driven home. He'd watch the blood drip off of him onto a rag; sitting on the mattress in the garage, the radio blasting classic rock, Arthur's endless party noise coming from the house and the night rains drumming on the roof. In the end, it wouldn't be enough. He had to be all that he could be. As soon as a batch finished in the shed he smoked from it, and all was well.

In the months he was at Arthur's, there were times when they arrived at the same place in their cycles of use. Once, they were both coming off a crash and Arthur came through the door from the house and sat on the steps leading down into the garage.

"Kid, bring me a hit."

Devin brought the bong over and handed it to the man without looking at him. After a deep draw and noisy hold, Arthur spoke.

"From the kids up at Lewiston?"

Devin leaned against a holed boat elevated on sawhorses. "Yeah, I guess."

"I can tell. Lousy shit. Some hippie dad growing it, no doubt."

Devin shrugged and kept his eyes down.

"Kid, how long has it been since you took a shower? I mean really. You know I said you could come in and do that. I said that didn't I?

"Yeah, you said it. And I've done it a few times. I try to wait 'til you're gone."

"Well, it's had to have been a long time. I mean, I've never seen anyone look like that. You're starting to scare the customers off."

"You see me every day."

"And usually I can't see straight at all. No work today until you shower. And none until you wash those clothes. All of your clothes! Don't wash them with anything of mine."

Arthur snickered a bit before he continued. "Do you miss your girlfriend?"

"Who?" Devin gave him just a flash of blue.

Arthur shook his head in wonder. "Never mind. Don't cook anything in the shed today."

"Ok."

The man put his elbow on his knee and supported his jaw with his hand, trying to assume a thoughtful pose.

"Look, Devin, I knew this guy, name of Lester Nicks. We partied hard together at one time. Son of a bitch hates me now, I'm sure, because I heard he found God or something. He takes a lot of pride in being sober I guess. Last month I saw the son of a bitch come into Nehats like he was riding on a donkey with people fanning leaves or something. One of my best customers got on the bus to Lewiston with him. Anyway, what I'm trying to say is, well, see, he's got these houses up there now where everybody goes straight and works shitty jobs and plays foosball and eats spaghetti out of big pots and shit. What I'm trying to say is that if you ever think you'd be better off with him than staying here, I don't know, I'd even buy your bus fare. Don't get me wrong, you can stay. But you know, this operation here, I like you and all, but there's no future in it for you."

Devin looked up. He opened his mouth, but if he was going to say something, he stopped. He turned and walked over to his tiny collection of extra clothes, which could have easily been mistaken for oily rags dropped on the garage floor. He put his hands up to his head, as if they could stop the thoughts. *'I have everything I need right here.' That's what you were going to say, wasn't it? This is heaven on earth.*

Arthur Childs stood up and turned to go back inside the house, then stopped and looked at him again. "You know what Nena, that hard core bitch that comes over to see me, said last night? She peeked out here and saw you and then she tells me, 'He's going to die here.' Man, I can't have you dying here." He shook his head and hit the bong again hard and then extended it back toward Devin, who didn't respond, so Arthur just set it on the steps and went inside.

23

The bust came in a swarm of oddly clad commandos; camouflage fatigues and bulletproof vests. The camo effect was canceled by the bright orange hazmat helmets with full breathing apparatus and white gloves. Most had automatic rifles, but a few had holstered pistols and carried crowbars. Arthur didn't put up a fight. There were hunting rifles and a pistol that he kept close because of his cash, but he had no intention of going out in a blaze of glory. One on thirty made bad odds, whereas they went to about even in the courtroom. Maybe this would give him a couple of years off from the party. Maybe his sister could come down from Seattle and keep the shop going.

Devin had used late the previous night, and hadn't slept at all when they came in at dawn. If he had been armed, he would have fought and died for nothing. It was like a video game, creatures attacking from all sides, he would blast at them and run for the high ground if he was armed. Instead, he ran toward the woods and right into two officers with weapons pointed at him.

Handcuffed and lying in the back of a police cruiser, Devin's mind raced with things real and unreal. Voices drifted in through the open window.

How did we not shoot that kid?

Thank God we didn't, I'd never get it out of my head.

I won't get him out of my head anyway.

Might have been a mercy killing, but I couldn't have lived with it.

***

His clothes were contaminated, so they incinerated all of them. He couldn't come close to filling the prison jumpsuit they got for him. He was like one of those Halloween decorations where the skeleton is loose in the clothes. For his protection, they had him in a private cell away from the others. An officer told him if he would give more information, Social Services would come in and help him. *Help do what?*

The deputy was a big strong woman. She had a clean, attractive face, a commanding voice, and couldn't sit. She paced the floor smiling, as if she was the luckiest person in the world to be able to debrief an uncooperative, twitching boy.

She brought him in to a meeting room, cuffed in front, and had him sit facing her as she moved from one wall to the other, arms folded, sighing several times before speaking. "So kid, Devin, they tell me you still won't talk about yourself."

Devin looked to the wall opposite of the one she was walking toward.

"Someone out there knows who you are. Someone misses you."

He didn't answer, but Deputy Judy was not deterred. "That's quite a set of eyes you have. Some real special peepers. Did you get those from your folks? I'll bet people always try to look at those don't they?"

Devin glanced at her with some curiosity, and then looked away.

"Did you ever do sports? You look like maybe you were a gymnast or something. But I'll bet you are not feeling real strong now."

He looked down to the floor then back up at her, but only at her midsection, not at her face.

"Please Devin. Just tell us your last name. Or give us the name of someone who knows you. Damn, my dog gives me more than this."

Devin became fascinated with the vast variety of things that Judy wore on her belt. Maybe more stuff than he'd ever owned in his life. And the variety of shapes and sizes of tooled leather compartments, that was something. He shook his head.

"Arthur says he doesn't know your last name. That you were partying there and he let you crash for a while. I don't believe him. Your prints haven't been matched to anyone. We'll send them for a more comprehensive search, but I'm not optimistic.

You won't be charged, but you can't stay here. You won't need a lawyer because we are not going to do anything to you except feed you, but not forever. Let me help you."

He looked up at her and made the decision to speak. "I can't go anywhere like this. No one can take me like this. I'd kill the few people I know just by showing up. Tell them I spit on you or something and I'll just stay here."

Judy moaned out of frustration and not a little pity. He kept staring at her unblinking, the odd social affect caused her to start pacing again. "How old are you?"

He was silent.

"How much methamphetamine do you use? You were still high when we got you."

Devin didn't feel strongly about protecting Arthur, but still, you don't just tell the whole story. "Too much."

"All the time?"

"I would if I could. But I haven't always been able to get it."

"You get it from Arthur."

"He has parties and it shows up. I won't talk more about it."

Judy shook her head and walked back toward Devin. "We're considering slavery charges against him."

"Slavery?" Devin looked confused.

"Of you, Devin."

He shook his head with a half smile. "No one owns me. I don't know what you're talking about."

"Maybe no person owns you, but something does. Doesn't it?"

That killed his smirk. "I want to stay here. I can stop if I stay here."

"We've got people here that will eat you all up, Devin, like the Big Bad Wolf. And you can't have that cell forever, what do you think this is, the Hilton?"

"If I tell you, you find my mother. Then I get sent there and I don't quit and it kills her and then my sisters will never see her again."

Judy tried not to show emotion, but her voice quivered and she had to restart her next comment. "What if I could get you committed somehow to a rehab?" She tried to sound confident when she said it. Devin had already heard, no criminal charges, no punishment, which is apparently what the state felt rehab was.

"What if I don't want to quit?"

"You just told me that if you stay here you would quit."

"If I stay here, I have to quit if I'm in a cell."

Judy pursed her lips and blew her air out softly. "All right. Let's go back to your grand suite."

It was there, looking out the bars, that Devin would find himself fixating on Braxton. He replayed every second of the season with Cardsen, Katie, Van Gorder, Overman and the Matchiks that he could remember, including the painful parts. Those pains paled in comparison to his current life. A couple of times each day, he looked and listened, and confident that no deputies were coming by to ogle him like at a zoo, he dropped for push-ups, and he even shot a few double leg takedowns against air.

Two days later Devin found himself in a sit down meeting with a judge, a district attorney, Judy, and Lester Nicks. Looking down, Devin shook hands with Lester, whom he had never met. Stealing glances at the man, he saw the rough face and tattooed hands. Lester didn't look official and his name sounded familiar.

The D.A. had a few papers spread out and a worried look on his face. "Highly unusual Les, I don't know. I don't think I can protect you from some liability here. You take a kid this young, it's the ultimate risk for you and your place. You know that."

"I wrote the letter there, I take full personal responsibility. His funding would come out of my personal trust, not the general fund for my homes, to protect them. One look at him and I know there is immediate hope. He hasn't lived a lifetime of this. Fast mover, fast down, and fast up I'm willing to bet. He can't be fifteen at the most. Register him with Social Services as Devin Doe. Have a social worker come out weekly to talk to him. And make sure they come, to cover all our asses. Medical every month or something. Check him any way you want.

"Wherever he comes from, he said he can't go back or it's the end of everyone in his life. I believe him."

The wrangling went on for another hour. Devin listened to very little. He stared at Judy's gun. All six bullets. If he could, he'd use all six bullets on himself. Appendage by appendage for five, and the sixth perpendicular through the scar on his head. Finally the judge and D.A. got up and left, and Judy seemed nervous as Les reached over and patted Devin's upper arm to get his attention.

"Devin, it's Les Nicks talking to you. I know you maybe forgot my name. You are going to come up to Lewiston and stay with us at a men's home. I'm excited to work with a kid so young. It might be scary at first but I promise to keep you safe. I used to be a tweaker myself, Devin, and I know it can be done."

Devin's head jerked up at the word tweaker. Maybe the guy was lying about the "used to be" part, maybe they actually cooked up there in secret. "What would we do there?"

"We get straight Devin. That's all."

24

"The Skidder."

Devin couldn't hear well enough so he moved the phone to his good ear and tried again. "Hello, I'm sorry, I didn't catch that."

"The Skidder. Is this the place that you wanted to call?" There was laughter and the clinking of glass. Bar sounds. A juke box played an ancient song he'd heard at Arthur's, *We Gotta Get Out of This Place.*

"Um, is there a woman there named Alexa?"

"She's working." Her voice was suspicious. "You want to talk to Frank?"

"No. Alexa, please. Tell her it's her son. Tell her boss I'm sorry to bother her at work."

"Her son."

"Yes ma'am."

"Ma'am! That's beautiful. Kid, if this is really you, she'll flip. Let me take my time, will you wait?"

"Please." He heard the phone clunk on the bar. He immediately received a foul conversation between two howling men, so he pulled the phone away a bit. Devin twisted and looked back down the hall toward the kitchen. Les was having a laugh with two of the guys and pretending too hard at not paying attention to Devin making the call.

"Devin? Are you there?" Her breathless voice held expectation and fear, as if she was calling out to a ghost that might actually respond.

"It's me, Mom."

"Oh my God." She took off speaking without taking a breath. "Devin, I don't know what to say, my heart is pounding.

Are you safe? Are you in trouble? Where are you? Oh, don't answer! I'm sorry, please, I don't know what to say. I'm just glad you called. I care about that more than any answers to questions. I love you, I miss you. I..."

Devin leaned a shoulder against the wall, his back to the kitchen so no one could see the tears on his cheeks. "Mom, I know. You don't know how good it is to hear your voice. And I'm safe. And trouble's been and gone mostly. Kimmy and Leza how are they, do you have any idea?"

His mom snorted, and whined. "We're visiting each other now. We have a deal with Social Services."

There was a pause. He knew that his mom was looking around for eavesdroppers.

"If I get to Medford, down by Grandma's, and check in there with the agencies and get a job, they'll let the girls move down there to me."

"What about Frank, he owns that place, right?" Devin made a fist and began to dig the knuckles into the scar on the side of his head. There would have to be the usual escape from a man, always the same. He didn't need to be there to know.

Alexa sighed. "We're breaking up. He knows I've got to get back to you kids and do it right. He won't try to stop me. Please, come down to Grandma's and we'll meet you there. Are you in Portland? We could go together."

"I'm in this place out on the coast with some people. It's a rehab, Mom. I'm sober almost six months. Tell Kimmy and Leza I've been the worst big brother, but I hope to see them."

"Oh, Devin." Her voice faltered. "I'm so happy you're there. What do we do now?"

"Just give me Grandma's number in Medford. I got to do some more work here, then I'll call there and see if you made it. Say, five, six weeks. Mom, try to go down. Get the girls back, you can do it if you try hard. Tell Kimmy and Leza I love them."

"Devin, where can I call you? Or at least please call me here again tomorrow. Please, Devin."

"No, Mom. Sorry, I can't. I won't call you at Skidder's anymore. I'll check Medford, ok?"

"Ok." He could barely hear her, she was so choked up.

There was a man's loud voice in the background. "Alexa, what the hell?"

Devin couldn't stand it, so he hung up. He sat on the floor of the hallway for several minutes, and Les and the others had sense enough not to come near.

* * *

"Would you like to do the affirmations one more time?"

Devin looked directly at Dr. Washburn. He liked looking at her. His therapist was an attractive thirty-nine year old with short black hair and blue eyes, almost as different as his own. She always looked him in the eyes and was genuinely excited when she asked him how things were going, as if he could possibly have anything exciting to tell about group home life and endless internal battles. Les was there with them for his last session, Devin had invited him. Devin wasn't reluctant to recite the themes that she and Les and all the guys had helped him build. For the hundred and something time, and last time in Lewiston, he related the creed that he would carry with him. "I'm ready."

Dr. Washburn gave him cues from the written affirmations. He didn't need them, but he liked that she was still here, ready to work for him and with him.

"Your choice."

"I have chosen to leave the life of drugs because I have gone as far as they could take me, and I have found nothing there that better informs me of who I am intended to be. I have built no fulfilling relationships during my time of use, and I've damaged several."

"Relapse."

"Relapse does not have to happen, but it is statistically likely. It is not the end. I must contact my sponsor immediately to discuss how to get back up."

"Sex."

Devin slid forward to the edge of his seat and squinted in concentration.

"Thinking of sex done with meth will be a powerful force in my mind. I know I will never experience that level of sensation again. I compare to the man who used to drive one hundred thirty on the highway. He remembers the thrill and doesn't deny it, but he has recognized its foolishness and does not need to repeat it to fulfill his life. In fact, it cannot be repeated. It will be best to meet a girl who moves very slow. I will need to allow myself to be touched. I will give affection and if needed, pretend to enjoy it until it becomes real. I remember that I have damaged others with my behavior."

"Your body."

"I have God-given athletic talent, still not fully realized. I can run and run. I believe I can wrestle and do other things. But I have a fine mind as well, and I have great potential for being educated. I can balance the needs of body and mind, and help each grow. I can deny a physical want for emotional and mental gain."

His demeanor remained detached, but he recited each word with intensity, with importance.

"The Other."

"I have always felt a presence inside of me, fighting this presence has contributed to my difficulties. I have not been able to identify or eliminate this presence. I accept it as part of myself. Serving others, mind, body, relationships, and communing with God eclipse the need of The Other."

"Relationships."

"Serving others is something I must practice. I must pursue sober relationships, beginning with my Mother and sisters who need me. As we both have addictions, I can allow my Mother the same space I've needed in mine, yet I can remain sober and help my sisters. I will have awkward times building relationships, people fear what they don't understand, but even the most awkward will be more real than those built through my addiction."

"Higher Power."

"A relationship with the Higher Power, who is manifest to me in His son Jesus Christ, will sustain me. I am blessed to have the ability to feel His presence. I am blessed to have been chosen to walk a difficult path while still young. I can endure great pain of many types with his comfort.

***

Later, at the bus stop, the guys who could get away from work, nine in all, were there to see him off. Les moved among them, not as a leader, but as a peer. Dr. Washburn was there, and Deputy Judy from Tillamook County. One by one they shook his hand or hugged him. He allowed Glendon to hug him the longest. He tried to feel something extra when the women hugged him, and while he couldn't honestly say he felt anything different physically, something seemed to strengthen his hope that he could someday build a full relationship with a female.

Les shook his hand. Tears poured out of the man's eyes and ran down his cheeks. The bus door was open and waiting. Devin didn't want to look at those tears, but he forced himself to anyway.

"I can't think of a worse sin than for me to ever wish to keep someone here when they are ready to go. But I think it's happening to me, so get the hell up on that bus."

"Give my spot to someone right away."

"That won't be any trouble, young man, they're everywhere."

"I'll send a wrestling schedule and results." He tossed the small travel bag they had given him over his shoulder and ran up the steps into the bus. They all stayed in one group and waved as the bus left. It was only then that it sank in that they all came to see him. Just him. He looked out the window and glimpsed the surf a half a mile away. He smiled. *That was a great beach to run on.*

25

March, 2003

The week after spring break, the year of the Braxton wrestling championship, Cardsen perched behind his teaching desk as the kids worked. The triangle formed by Devin, Steven, and Katie Gutierrez was still there, changed in minor ways since the fall.

Devin had an aisle seat near the front so they could keep subtle eye contact and ease intercepting each other after class. That happened less now, and Devin didn't smile or talk wrestling much anymore. Still, when Cardsen glanced over, he sometimes caught Devin looking away quickly because he had been staring at his coach. When Cardsen told a good story, Devin would laugh and look all around the room at the other kids laughing. For Cardsen, that was the best. They interacted during work time because Devin's grade consisted only of those things that Cardsen could cajole him into attempting during class. He tried to call Devin's mother, but she didn't call back.

The kid was the laughing stock of the teacher's lounge. Hilariously low grades, the smell of him, and were those pine needles in his rat's nest of hair? Sociopath. Feral dog.

He could be so cute and pathetic at times that someone might want to take him home, they'd say while chewing on a cracker, *then you realize he'd put a hatchet through your head some night.* The last piece had to be added for the laughter of those there. And to Cardsen, it seemed they all loved to bring it up when he was around. The dark humor of cops and ambulance drivers and rest home orderlies and junior high teachers. Same old shit. Cardsen knew all about that stuff, used to participate in it all the time. No longer.

Steven now had the right front corner of the triangle. He didn't cry anymore. His mouth was a cynical closed slash. His other grades at school were in free-fall but in Cardsen's class he held a high B. The grade for Cardsen stood as a thank you and an I-owe-it-to-you. *I'm done with the rest of them, but not just yet with you.* On one side of his three-ring notebook, under the clear plastic sheath, was his gold colored embossed wrestling certificate with "Area Champion" in bold print. The other side of the notebook held a well developed sketch of a mushroom, and a block of Slim Shady lyrics. Cardsen wasn't interested in what they said.

At the apex of the triangle was Katie. Cardsen kept her there so she wouldn't have to twist her neck to look at Steven. She still looked, but spring was her turn to cry. Steven had hurt her, of that Cardsen was sure. Stupid kid, silly, stupid kid for doing that. He watched her until the bell rang a minute later. "Katie, could you stay a minute?" The class, including Steven and Devin, filed out. Cardsen tried to make his request seem casual. Katie stopped near his desk. With her books held tight to her chest, her face revealed turmoil and an adolescent search for the proper expression.

When the last of the kids left, Cardsen made eye contact with her. Digging into the secret love life of kids was one thing that could make Cardsen feel awkward, and holding that eye contact became difficult. "Katie, hey, well, um, I wanted to ask you something. I want you to understand that you only need to answer if it's ok with you, because I'm not sure if I should ask. But well, anyway, I couldn't help but notice this year how much you wanted to be friends with Steven. Now I see him struggling, and I see you struggling. And sad."

She broke eye contact and looked down a bit. "We were friends. Kind of starting in wrestling season. He called me some. One time he walked me home from school, and he had me laughing the whole way."

Tears began to run down her brown cheeks. Cardsen shifted his butt in his seat and felt untethered and unprotected. *This could be a dumb thing to do.* "I saw you at the Valentine's dance with him."

"It was a date. He asked me to it. My parents drove us. His mom was supposed to pick us up. The dance was so much fun. You wouldn't believe how sweet and funny and smart he can be. It turned out that he never told her to pick us up. He wanted me to walk all the way to this guy named Jensen's house.

"I told him no, and he tried to talk me into it for awhile. I just said I would call my parents from the pay phone outside." Katie was talking very fast now, and Cardsen sensed she had paused for a breath, not for him to talk. "So he asks me for a kiss, and we did. Then we went around the corner of the building for another one. He just changed there while we did that." She glanced up at Cardsen's eyes.

"He grabbed me all over. He pressed me to the bricks and I kind of had to wrestle free, and then he did it again. The second time I pushed him away I stepped back out in to the light. I was so angry. I couldn't believe it. I shouted at him and called him an asshole. I went to the pay phone and called my parents and they could tell I was upset. After the call I walked back around to see if he was still there. He was on his knees on the little patch of grass there. He bent over almost flat to the ground and had his arms up over his head like he used to do in class last fall, with his forehead clear to the grass." She lifted her arms to demonstrate. Her tears had dried up.

"It had started to rain again, hard, and he didn't move. He never moved. My parents came in a few minutes. I checked a couple of more times before they got there and he never moved from there and he didn't know I watched him. When my parents picked me up, they asked about him. I told them we had a silly argument, and that he decided to ride with friends."

"Katie," Cardsen paused to gather his speech, trying to focus his concern only on her. "I'm proud of you. You made such a good decision. I'm sorry that you went through that, the disappointment must hurt. I think he has things going on in his mind that make him less able to do what you and I know are the right thing. Maybe someday, but not today, not this year. I am so sorry.

"If I keep trying with him, if you see me with him, will you know that I would never condone that kind of behavior or imply to him that it's cool?"

Katie shook her head. "I know you wouldn't. I know you want to help him."

She began to cry again and then continued to speak. "I want to help him, too. I still think of him on the ground not moving. Was he sorry or psycho? I don't understand. I've wanted to talk to him about it all, but I just feel so different now. Like he wanted to come and get from me what is important to hold back. I mean, like my parents say about that stuff, *'Kids at fourteen, ridiculous!'* A couple of times it looked as if he was going to talk to me, but he just walks away. And I do the same to him. Now it's been weeks and weeks."

"Katie, if you will listen to me for one piece of advice, only offered because it is so important. As much as compassion drives you, do not try to help Steven. The risks for you are much too high. I promise, I won't abandon him, and I will always try to bring as much help to his life as I can figure out. Maybe, just maybe, down the road, I might be talking years here, you will be friends. Reaching out to him now from your position, you might as well grab a high voltage line.

"The last thing I want to do when you have shown so much trust in me is threaten you Katie, but I am going to make a minor threat. If I see you not protecting yourself in your dealings with Steven, I'll go to your parents with this story, and I will do it because you are so important to me."

She looked at him, eyes serious, and shook her head. "Don't worry about me. If there was anything else I was willing to try, I would have tried it already."

26

Late in the year of the championship season, Cardsen ran into Jensen in the school parking lot. The happy-go-lucky partier was changing into a dark and fleeting character. Jensen's designer clothes were gone now for a darker look of black on black, and he had been in and out of school for several mysterious suspensions.

More than once Cardsen had seen Jensen's dad coming in to berate the administration. The dad delivered inane statements such as: "Quit picking on him." and "Why in the hell don't you have something positive he can get involved in?" and "He's supervised ALL of the time at home." and "Maybe if he wasn't so goddamned bored by all the people here."

One thing Jensen did have was Steven Matchik, and more recently acquired, Devin Thomsen. Alan Matchik and Gary Overman were now flirting with that scene as well. Cardsen often saw himself as an awkward, poorly placed impediment to the long slide of his boys.

As Cardsen made his way to his truck, he nearly bumped into Jensen cutting an odd angle across the lot.

"Hey, Cardsen." The kid made quick eye contact and stopped for an instant, looking for a quick way around the man to regain his path.

Cardsen tried to decide whether to talk to him. To say he had developed resentment for the kid would be an understatement. At the same time, there was that old urge of Cardsen's to reach out to Jensen. Cardsen couldn't lay it all on him, when Steven and Devin and the others had so many positive options they could have pursued. There was track, and freestyle wrestling at the high school, and hanging out with kids like Ryan Van Gorder or Katie Gutierrez. They could have come over to their coach's place to help him build and organize a new work area in his garage. All those things had been offered, but with Jensen is where they wanted to be. Cardsen spoke just in time to stop him again. "Jensen, I want you to tell me something."

"Yeah?"

"You've made some choices I don't agree with this year, but I think you're going to learn from them. In fact, something tells me you are going to be all right in the end. That's what I hope for."

Jensen stared at him, curious, Cardsen tossing him some love.

"But why did you hook in to Steven and Devin? You know they are wilder than you'll ever be, that they'll go farther."

"Hey, whoa." Jensen put up his hands as if to fend off something. "Cardsen, you are full of shit, you know that? You set me up then kick me in the nuts. You think I'm some sort of missionary recruiter? They walked to me, they knocked on my door."

Cardsen's jaw set tight and he clenched his fists, but he didn't say anything.

Jensen had a disarming smile, but there was anger in his eyes, and he moved closer to Cardsen, not intimidated. "You know why, *Coach*? Because I help them more than *you* do. I *want* to help them more than you do, I *can* help them more than you do, and I *do* help them more than you.

"You know nothing about stopping pain, you only call for more. You know nothing about making them important. You should see how important they are at my place." The boy gestured widely with his arms, then pointed at Cardsen. "You know nothing about showing them a different world. They create their own world now. You should see them laugh and have fun. Have you ever seen that? They're funny as hell, by the way."

Jensen pulled back, and then walked past, giving a wide berth. Then he slowed again and glanced back at the Coach. He had a superior smile, and a look of pity. "Don't worry Coach, they still love you. And sometimes they think you're funny, too."

27

Devin scanned everything from the moment he walked into Jensen's house. It was his third or fourth time there, and he still couldn't believe the size of the place. He studied all, the wooden pillars, the vaulted ceiling, the art work, the glass coffee table in the sitting room to his left. Just three people lived there, Jensen, his dad, and a twenty-four year old sister that Devin never saw. He kept his hands pushed down in the front pockets of his jeans. The pounding inside him was relentless. As Steven led him forward, he tossed head bobs to a few people he recognized. The hallway, decorated with Chinese vases and mirrors, led to a huge open kitchen with a hard tile floor and a bar with a sink and stools.

Three girls and five boys, older than Devin and Steven, stood by the barstools. The girls screeched annoying laughter as two of the guys raced on a double shot of some kind of liquor.

One of the better looking girls, Rennie, howled in delight when she saw Steven and Devin and left the others to join the newcomers. They met near the top of the stairs that led down to the game room. "Steven Matchik! It's everybody's lucky night now. Everyone was just asking about the guy that can walk on his hands."

Steven blew a little air out of the side of his mouth and smirked in response.

She edged up close to Steven, the beer bottle incongruous to her cute young face, and body that was still changing. She was at least two inches taller than the boy, and nearly two years older. The girl tossed her brown hair and reached over and stroked Devin's now clean but still unkempt mane.

"I see you brought your little friend again. Is this bleached? I mean no one is that blonde, are they?"

When she touched him, Devin's back arched like a cat. He panicked that he would get excited to the point everyone would notice, so he pulled a hand out of his pocket to dangle in front of his jeans.

Steven turned and smiled at Devin. "You're jumpy as hell!" he said. Then he studied Rennie a bit, like he was trying to decide something about her.

She breathed deeply and stared back. "Steven, could we talk tonight? I think we have a couple of more things we could talk about that we didn't get to last time."

Even with his inexperience, Devin could decipher what was going on. His eyes widened involuntarily as he looked from her face to Steven's. Steven smiled again and finally spoke to her. "Rennie, for sure I'll talk to you later, if you think you can wait awhile. Or you could come downstairs with us and see what else Jensen's got."

"Naw, my brother is picking me up, and he doesn't mind if he smells some beer, but if he smells that on me, he might come in here and go nuts."

"There's more than one thing down there." He looked her up and down.

Devin hung on every word, and recalled how someone told him a woman would thrash on you like a crazed animal after a snort or two of coke.

"You know what Steven?" She looked uncomfortable and slurred a bit as she tried to put something together. "I don't think, I mean, maybe you should slow...ah, um, you know what?"

"What?"

"You need to stop looking at me that way, that's what."

He grinned at her. "I'll talk to you later."

She walked away.

Steven turned to Devin. "God forbid she should smell like a little weed to her brother. She can reek of beer from slopping it down with these guys, she can walk bowlegged after our little talk, but God forbid she smell like a little weed."

Devin shrugged and looked to the floor. "Do you want to go down?"

Jensen and the others crowded on two facing couches, laughing and shouting and passing a bong. One guy, older than high school, leaned with his arm extended against the wall. He watched the boys smoke pot, like it was a spectator sport.

"Level five? Level *five*? Are you kidding? You are such a pussy. That's like slow moving gargoyles and shit." Jensen looked up from his rant and saw them coming down the stairs

"Hey! Steven! And the wild man, too. Get over here and check this out! Wait 'til we reload some fresh, just wait, and then you guys can go first."

One of the boys on the couch countered that. "Those little assholes, what have they ever done for us? Maybe they can bring something sometime."

The young man against the wall followed them to the group and sat next to Steven on the couch opposite Devin. He put a hand on Steven's shoulder and glared at the boy who had spoken. "This is my little brother, in whom I am well pleased. Shut your hole or you'll have to go through me."

Devin looked at their protector, Barnes, the one who brought the coke they did last week. He glanced at Steven, who was staring at him, like he was reading his mind. Devin remembered how things went after he did the first line of his life. Barnes said, "Look at that! The kid's a natural!" For hours, Devin laughed and wanted to roughhouse with Steven. They went back to Steven's house to sleep, but they didn't sleep until morning. In the middle of the night, Devin went into Alan's room and jumped on him and wrestled him. Then he and Steven talked and talked about a lot of things. He didn't know he could have a conversation like that. When Steven asked him how he liked the coke, Devin said it freed him. He smiled and stared back until Steven had to look away.

When they woke at eleven the next day, they went to the kitchen for food and Steven's mother asked him a couple of stupid questions about his family that he couldn't answer. She shook her head and walked out. The roar came on strong inside and he bolted for home. His mom told him she was so glad he was making nice friends like the Matchiks to spend time with. Devin went back to his room and sat at his little desk. He grabbed a pencil and fixated on sticking it through his eye. Instead, he called Steven and they went back over to Jensen's and did a bong load. After that, he returned home and slept until five.

On the couches at Jensen's, the group laughed and smoked. The mix of classic rock and rap blared and they shouted comments about the songs. A couple of Jensen's friends found inspiration to detail sex stories to the audience.

"Good shit, gents. I say, this is good shit!" Jensen drew a couple of snickers with his fake British accent as he passed the bong. "Steven, did you teach Rennie a lesson before you came down here? I've been working on her for months, and you come in last week and the next thing I know you got her moaning up in my sister's room. Don't shake your head. Rick heard it through the bathroom wall. Tell us about it."

***

Steven looked at the faces around him, only Jensen smiled now. The mention of he and Rennie shut Jensen's friends down. Steven didn't belong there. Fine. He didn't like any of them.

Only Jensen wanted him in the house. "Nothing to tell. She makes a lot of noise just talking."

"Yeah. And maybe I'll get your old squeeze, the Mexican puta, howling like a coyote sometime. Or maybe whistling through the hole in her lip." That brought the laughter back.

Time passed before Steven could assemble emotion through the thick buzz he had on. For a moment he fixated on Devin, those blue irises widened in surprise to the size of nickels, with a tiny black dot in the middle. Devin remained silent, his body shrunken almost out of sight between two bigger guys.

Jensen is talking about Katie Gutierrez. I should kill him. He tried to find the elusive anger required. In the humming of his mind, Steven found another thought instead. *Their insults are nothing compared to the way I treated her.*

At last, his body took action. Steven bolted up off the couch and across the room putting fists up to the side of his head.

The group could not connect the belated nature of the action to anything.

"What's wrong with that little dipshit?" someone said.

Steven touched his forehead to the wall. *She should date Ryan Van Gorder. He is straight and such a good guy. He'll wrestle at State in high school. She is so cool. They will be perfect. I'll tell Ryan the next time I see him. It was a good thing that Katie found out what being with Steven Matchik was really like.*

It was a good thing she found out.

Steven turned from the wall and there was Devin. *That kid didn't fit in either. When he arrived for the wrestling season, Devin was the biggest hit. Everyone jabbered about him; alien, angel or animal, depending on who you talked to. No one else moved like that on the mat. Now he's just an asshole, same as me. Austin Reichs said Devin was like a little dog someone beat for hours with a belt. Reichs said he'd seen an uncle do that before, and afterward the dog became jumpy, just like Devin.*

Ryan Van Gorder saw something else in Devin, shining light.

If he shines out light, that doesn't matter, because I absorb it.

What would Coach Cardsen think about all this? The man hounds me. I hate that. If he quit hounding me, I guess I'd hate that, too. Cardsen sure likes Devin. He'd want me to take him to the library or bowling or something.

Devin said the coke freed him. It freed me.

"You all right?"

Steven heard Devin speaking to him, but he didn't answer. Then he heard Barnes.

"You guys loved it last week, didn't you? That rush, that feeling of being right with yourself, of going on forever, yeah, I know all about that." Barnes was thin, with scraggly, random hair on his face and buzz-cut hair on his head. Acne dotted his face, crossed by a couple of scars that might hold a story. Easily four or five years older than Steven and Devin, he carried an expression of experience and knowing. He folded his arms and leaned back against the wall with one leg up, cigarette dangling out of the corner of his mouth.

The boys stood in front of him, hands in their back pockets.

"I could see how you guys liked it. Some of us, we were born for it, you know? But I've got to tell you, I got none to give you tonight."

Steven responded while Devin just looked down to the floor. "We couldn't pay you anyway."

Barnes pulled his cigarette out of his mouth and blew smoke at them. "I'm not worried about that shit. I just want to see happiness in this world, know what I'm saying? Listen, if you like that, I can take you so far past that. Blow your fucking mind.

"It takes balls though." He took another long pull. "Listen, let's get out of this wanna-be rich-kid playpen. You don't belong here. You guys have balls. You want to grab something better. Ride with me. I'll take you to a friend, and you won't believe it, just won't believe it. You down?"

Steven looked over at Devin who stared back at him, but neither spoke.

***

They arrived at the dark parking lot of RiverFest Park. The rain and overcast skies broke three weeks before, bringing an unusual spring. The air was crisp, but just tolerable in a T-shirt, if you were a kid. They set out walking across the festival grounds and took the dirt trail for runners and fishermen into the trees. The trees swallowed the ambient light from the subdivisions by I-205 and they plunged into the darkness, Barnes leading the way. In about two minutes, they could hear the Clackamas River up ahead. With their eyes adjusted to the dark, they could tell their trail would soon bend parallel to the river and out into the relative open. Just before the trees stopped, they were startled by someone who stood up suddenly on an old stump and stretched his arms to the sky.

"What's up?" The figure groaned as he stretched, as if he had just been awakened.

"It's Barnes."

"Barnes? What's up?"

"Just bringing some friends down. We want to party."

"So do I, but it's my turn to watch tonight. No problem though, I'm fixed up for later. Barnes, it's going to be an incredible summer. What the hell, did you bring hobbits?" The lookout laughed at his own joke.

"Some friends. They're cool. No bullshit posing. They just like to get high. They're just here to learn."

"Whatever, but aren't they a little young?"

"They're my friends."

Suddenly, Steven felt like running. He wanted to run all the way home and sleep in the same room with his brother Alan. He closed his eyes tight and crossed his arms to rub his shoulders.

He was afraid, part of him wanted it to end now before it started. Barnes was right about him not posing. He never bragged about what he used to anyone, didn't make it a tool to be cool. Barnes spoke right about the other half as well, more than being afraid, more than his warm home, he wanted to be high.

He wanted to be higher than he'd ever been before. He wanted to know his place, to stare at the sky and know that insignificance was ok and harmonious. His body flowing into it, indistinguishable. The mushrooms had done that some, and the coke had driven him hard toward it in a different way. What else was out there?

***

Devin shook all over, not out of fear, but from the growling and pounding inside of himself, a roar louder than the river. Images flashed of everything he had learned through his life about drug abuse. All the nonsense he had seen. Roy screaming and punching holes in the wall, scattering them to closets or outside. His mother naked and comatose on her bed, door left open. He used to feel a spike of pain thinking about what he had seen, now he was numb. At elementary school, when the cops talked baby talk about drugs, he couldn't look at anyone in his embarrassment. After last weekend, he was in shock for two days as it sunk in that he had done cocaine.

He was in the club now, in it with Roy and Cracker and the men back in LaGrande, in it with his mother.

All just a tease, wrestling at Braxton, Coach Cardsen, all the nice guys on the team, and Katie. Who was he kidding? He was a different species. And the coke wore off quickly and he didn't feel addicted and it freed him and he loved it and whatever it was they were after tonight better get him ahead of what was inside of him the way the coke had.

Under the wide concrete bridge there were five blankets spread out and the shadows of six or seven people dancing in the flickering light of a small open-flame camping stove. A couple of the shadows were female, but the boys didn't take much notice. If that was what they were after, they would have stayed at the party.

A man hunched over near the flame, a blanket over his shoulders; the medicine man, the war-chief, the teacher.

Barnes announced them and they were motioned over. The man called them brothers and had them sit down. He began to teach them in the flickering light. His love of craft would make one think he was a grizzled native showing how to twine a bone harpoon on a shaft with sinew. Gently, with love, his skeletal hands those of a master, he showed them how to set it up. How to melt it, collect it and inhale it just right out of the pipe. Deliberate and efficient the hands moved and his voice spoke with a detached love and gentle encouragement.

***

For a moment before he brought it to his mouth, Steven thought about his family. What they had shared seemed now like ancient history. He flexed his forehead and pinched his eyes shut to think about the future. Something in there might tell him to put on the brakes. He tried and tried but he couldn't even imagine light chasing the curtains of darkness on either side of the bridge and bringing the next day. There was something in his mind about a boy that looked like him, an athlete, people cheering, a girl taking his hand.

But that was someone else.

***

Devin thought about the river below them. He would go in only once, his hair streaming above him in the cold water. He would hold his breath until he let go and the water would rush in his lungs and he would thrash and panic and have visions of good things. Toys in his hands and his mom's smile as she tickled him and running and Cardsen flipping a steak on to his dinner plate next to the Bible Reverend Tim Burgess gave him, and a referee raising his hand. Then the thing inside him would be done and defeated.

But what if then he was somehow still conscious when he was dead, and trapped with only it and himself forever in the water?

He looked over at Steven. He had a friend. He was staying with his friend.

It took a few minutes to work, but when it did, the world changed. It gave everything it was supposed to give. They say it releases ten times what your first orgasm does, and then it goes on and on. An exponential leap past what evolution has set as a species-preserving excitement level. A sense of well-being bestowed on them, a rightness with creation that seemed as if it would never end.

***

For once, each boy moved in a unified mind and body, with one master, and each boy had no schisms to contend with.

28

August, 2003

Months had passed since the Championship. Summer in Oregon peaks around Labor Day, and a place known for rain becomes a desert. Outside, the grass burned to khaki. Inside, Cardsen sweated in his classroom, waiting for his first class of the year. He had a foot up on his desk and his hands behind his head. Cardsen knew great things would happen, as in every year. But the previous months had taken their toll.

In the spring, Steven drifted away from him. When summer vacation arrived, he disappeared. A letter came the day before school, from the county juvenile lock-up. Steven kept it brief, just a single paragraph, a faint contact as he did two weeks in juvie. A bag of pot fell out of his coat pocket in front of a cop doing security at the River Festival in June. By the time Cardsen figured out how to have a visitation, Steven was released and already skipping probation appointments. Information was slim; Steven's mother didn't return his calls.

There were the rumors of Gary Overman doing crazier and crazier things, fighting with his parents and following Steven around during the summer.

Devin Thomsen, how could he even think about that kid? What Cardsen saw in the summer traumatized him, a fog suffocating his spirit, so he blocked the image out.

They were all gone from him now, off to high school. Who knew if they'd even try high school? Cardsen's memories of the team hung in his mind like a beautiful painting of a dead brother.

Cardsen had done what he must do, steel himself against the pain and prepare for the next batch. He had Alan coming back.

Alan would be in his class and on the mat. *"I'm going to lead this team." "I know."* Alan cast as the perfect blank slate to correct missed opportunities, and to write his influence, and other such high drama. To hell with self-doubts about his ability to coach the kids and his fear of what the year could bring. Alan would be the conduit of information about the others, together they would pull the boys back together, get them all the help they needed.

Cardsen succeeded in putting on his normal first day act: authority, touch of humor, organization. Beginning that day, every move he made has to be about getting in their heads, whether they know it or not. Outflank them, outsmart them. They are cared about, valued, and their best hope is to knuckle under to the plan.

The show came off well, but as the day wore on, Cardsen went to autopilot. Period after period, he picked up the roll sheets and the name never appeared. In the hall during each passing time, he looked for Alan. Nothing, just a pit forming in his stomach. What the hell? A scan of the cafeteria at lunch, nothing. The anxiety that his wife, Sonia, had helped him battle in recent months began to return. When the day was over, he headed straight for Student Services. Jill, the department secretary, gave him a broad smile and tossed him a sucker.

"How was day one, Sean?"

"Standard. First day number eleven for me, by six periods, that's sixty six times. The faces change, but..." Jill's eyes were glazing over, so he paused, and restarted. "Hey, I'm trying to find out what's up with Alan Matchik. I thought he was supposed to be in my class.

"Alan Matchik? He didn't finish registering. Two days ago, when you guys were in meetings, his parents came and withdrew him."

Cardsen grimaced and his body jerked as if he'd been punched in the stomach. Jill finished quietly and her face now showed great concern.

"Withdrew."

"Yes."

"Just like that. No warning."

"Sean, it's a pretty big school, happens all the time."

"Did you say parents? As in plural?"

"Well, it was his mom, and I assumed it was his dad, but then again, weren't they divorced or something?"

"Shit."

Jill's face contorted further and she tried to catch him directly in the eyes. "Sean, I'm sorry. I should have remembered how much you were in here about them last year and-"

"Forget about it, Jill. It's not your fault. You can't remember everybody's little hobbies."

"Hang in there, Sean."

Cardsen had already spun out the door and strode down the hall, feeling three inches shorter than when he came in. He went right into the department office and dug into his files for the number. He knew he should probably wait and calm down, but he figured he couldn't afford to let this go further if he could have an effect. Would she even answer?

"Hello, Mrs. Matchik, this is Sean Cardsen at Braxton."

"MIS-ter Cardsen. So nice of you to call. And by the way, it's Karen Glosser now."

Cardsen searched to read the tone in her voice, but he couldn't pin it down, it was as if she was coming from eight different directions, half positive and half negative. "I just found out Alan is not at our school, and well, I'm surprised. I was wondering if there was any information you felt ok sharing with me about the boys, in particular, this immediate situation with Alan."

"I'm certain that you'll be able to fill that spot on your wrestling team and-"

"Mrs. Matchik, Ms. Glosser, I'm sorry to interrupt you, but it really doesn't have much to do with that. I feel like Alan and I had developed a nice friendship and an important relationship and-"

"He's thirteen years old, Mr. Cardsen. And I don't plan on losing another one in the public schools."

Cardsen sat silenced by her suddenly clipped tone. *Yeah, of course it's the school's fault.* Unable to respond, he simply waited to see if she was going to continue.

When she did, it was with a minor level of contrition. "Sean," she called him for the first time ever by that name, "I'm sorry, that wasn't fair to you. We appreciate all you have done. You have been very special to my boys. But Alan needs a new direction, and he is not going to find it there. Look, there is a new Starbucks near the corner of Pine and 201. My fiancé and I are meeting there at five this afternoon, could you join us? I'd like you to meet him and have him help me explain this. He has played a big role in this new understanding."

Have to go. If I ever want to be called upon for anything again, I'll have to go. "Well, I have football, but I'll leave it to my assistant early and see you there Ms. Glasser."

"Glosser."

"Right."

***

"Black coffee? That's all?"

Alan and Steven's mother looked a bit more subdued in dress and makeup than Cardsen remembered her, and her hair was pulled back tightly in a ponytail. She smirked at the cup he carried, and the man with her extended a hand.

"Coach Cardsen, I've heard a lot about you. I'm Todd."

The man's name was utterly unimportant to Cardsen. The fiancé gripped his hand, trying to be firm, emitting in every vibration the recognition and reaction to how much smaller he was than the coach. Suburban macho. Late forties. Scrubbed Promise Keeper manliness in a tieless button down shirt. Thin light brown hair swooped sideways in an unmoving coif, slacks with a cell phone case prominent on the belt. Hint of aftershave or cologne.

"Well, hopefully you haven't heard everything." *I wonder how his first family turned out?* Mused Cardsen.

Todd looked at him suspiciously but covered with a smile and the three of them sat down. Afterward he looked the coach up and down and spoke. "Did you come over from football practice?"

"Yeah, it was a good night to leave early, we worked them pretty hard."

Todd smirked a bit. "You get paid for that?"

Cardsen ground his rear on the chair below him. *Don't show it on your face.* "A bit. Extra duty you know. I'm a science teacher for what pays the bills."

"Ah, evolution and all that."

"Sometimes."

Now Cardsen couldn't help but let his eyes bore into the other man's, and the man looked down to his napkin.

"Well… I've been grinding out a long one at the warehouse. We're a publisher. The best of Christian books. Lots of new stuff coming out. Got to move hard every day, no government support or government hours there, know what I mean?"

Cardsen didn't answer, but stared, and the man wouldn't look at him.

"I should send you books from some alternative scientists."

Karen Glosser steered the conversation at that moment. For that small favor Cardsen was glad.

"Mr. Cardsen, we've placed Alan in Columbia Christian Academy. Isn't it a wonderful opportunity?"

He just loved it when people ended with a question like that. Agree and violate what you believe, or disagree and end your finger hold on your source of information. Like any deft conversationalist, he ignored the stupid question and moved on. "Is this something Alan has wanted to do?"

As soon as Cardsen finished, Todd Whatever was talking. That was the longest he could stay out of it. "He's struggling with it right now. His heart is not in a good place. He needs to open his heart to Christ. Are you a Christian, Mr. Cardsen?"

"Well, um, yes, I try to be. I mean, I may not match in everything that you-"

"Have you opened your heart to Christ, Mr. Cardsen?"

Ok, damn me to Hell, God, but I want to break this guy's neck already, and I bet Alan does, too. "I didn't come to discuss the nuances of my Christianity. I'd like to keep the focus on Alan."

The man looked away once again, and took an audible breath before speaking. "Alan is a wonderful boy, but so scarred by his father, so let down by his brother." The fiancé was shaking his head before continuing, coif unmoved. "We found out that he was experimenting in similar ways to Steven, and hoping to stop it before he finds the Hell that Steven has, we enrolled him in a Christian rehab camp until mid-September. Then he will return here and start late at the Academy."

Cardsen stole a quick glance at Karen. She looked up from her latte and nodded knowingly with tight lips, eyes tired. *She's turned it all over to this guy already. Screw it. Waste of time now. Get as much information as possible and bolt.*

And sink a couple of digs into them.

Christian Rehab camp? There's such a thing? Ah, well, anything beats being with Steven or Devin Thomsen right now.

Cardsen broke eyes with the man and looked back to Karen. "Does Alan have contact with his father?"

Todd crossed his arms and went quiet. To her credit, she didn't react as much and gave a look that was philosophical.

"He has tried a few times this past year to get back in touch. He took Alan to lunch three times this past month and then went over to visit Steven at juvie last week. But he ignored the boys in their most crucial time, and he seems committed to perpetuating his sinful lifestyle. So I have the responsibility to protect them from that. They haven't been willing to listen to him anyway. Recently, Alan has been talking about running off to stay with him, and even his father says that is a bad idea right now. Their father is very unsettled."

"No kidding. The gay promiscuity level is beyond belief." added Todd, shaking his head.

Cardsen bored in with his eyes, and tried to keep away a smirk as he looked at the man. "Wow, Mr. Matchik told you that?"

Karen interjected quickly before Fiancé could answer. "He just said it is no place for a kid right now, but that he wants Alan to visit and eventually work something out so both boys can come to Seattle more often."

Get useful information. Cardsen tried to look down at his coffee thoughtfully. "Could I write to Alan at this camp?"

Karen shook her head. "He can only accept letters from me. I'll have him call you when he gets home and let you know how it's going."

Cardsen knew that wouldn't happen. He had tried to call Alan several times during the summer, using the pretense of wrestling camp for both Steven and Alan at the high school. They never responded.

Of course, it could have been Alan hiding his sliding condition. Steven had done that, desperate to interact with him when Cardsen could catch him, but never making the initial contact. *Kids in trouble, they won't talk to you when they need it the most, don't want to disappoint, afraid they'll be seen for what they are. Then they show up when they are on an upswing, pretending that the cloud that trails above and behind them can't be seen.* In juvenile detention, Steven sobered up a bit and wrote the short letter.

"Steven has written me already."

"I know he has. He told me that."

"He writes great letters. He could be a writer."

Karen showed no emotion at the shift to her older son, she didn't even nod or acknowledge the compliment to him. Not encouraged, Cardsen nevertheless pressed on.

"I'm in no position to tell you what to do, but I do believe that Braxton Junior High and wrestling are very important things in Alan's life. I hate to see him lose the opportunity for success, be part of something bigger than himself, and continue some good friendships. You know, the kids on the team right now live clean, and I sure do care about him and Steven. I mean, they have become a big part of my life."

Fiancé Todd began to speak, but Karen sighed and waved him quiet. Then she gave Cardsen a hard look. "Sean, please. Are you blind? Your intentions are good. But I have one son that spent two years under your wing, and he is doing stuff beyond anything I could have imagined. That is what you've inadvertently sanctioned in your sports."

Cardsen sat stunned at the verbal assault. He couldn't even begin to build a comeback.

"And to encourage my boy to have a friendship with that freak white trash that moved in, the Thomsen kid, it's unconscionable that you unleashed that criminal on our kids without checking him out. A drug addict. My God. Just months after your blessed influence, and that close team, Steven is addicted and has been incarcerated. How could you let that little blonde demon near our kids?"

She would always hold the keys to finding Steven and Alan. He couldn't let the bridge burn over her anger. He remained empathetic to her pain. After all, she had probably shed more tears and lost more sleep than he had, and that was plenty. But the recasting of Devin Thomsen in her version, her absurd tapestry of the last ten months, that could not be allowed to stand. *If she saw Devin now, the way he recently had, she'd know there were things she couldn't possibly imagine.*

"Mrs. Matchik, you do know that Steven had been attending unsupervised parties for several months before he brought Devin Thomsen along, don't you? Devin Thomsen is every bit as important to me…"

"I'm not 'Mrs. Matchik.'"

Todd stood up. "I think you should go, Coach Cardsen."

"Probably." Cardsen stood up and looked back and forth between the couple. Karen did not make eye contact with him. "If you have a change of heart, please call me."

"Nothing is bigger than Christ, Coach Cardsen, certainly not you or your team. You need the change of heart." The man looked so smug. Cardsen thought about hitting him so hard that he would fly into the display of overpriced barista supplies.

"You're not 'Mrs. Matchik,' either." It was the lamest of comebacks, but Cardsen liked it anyway, and he left.

***

Sonia rubbed Cardsen's back lightly after he sat up in bed and put his legs over the side. He had been fighting the tears for a half an hour, and then he just let them come, no sobbing, just giant drops that formed and spread on his upper cheeks. Embarrassed, he kept his back to her, though it was obvious. He blew his nose.

Sonia sighed. "Maybe if it doesn't work out, they'll bring him back to Braxton. Or, maybe it will work for him at that other school."

"I guess. But it's more than that. It's piling up. All three of them, I've lost all three of them in a few months. And who knows about Overman? I hope I can do better with our own kids."

"You haven't lost anybody, Sean. What must it mean to Steven to be able to write you? What other adult is he stepping up to write? Alan will get in touch someday, you'll see. And our kids, I'm not worried a bit, not with their father here. That woman is confused. She has no clue about who is playing what role in this tragedy."

She poked him playfully in the back. He sighed and relaxed some.

"Devin Thomsen," he said. Another round of tears forced their way out against his will when he choked out the name.

It was Sonia's turn to sigh. "Sean, the world is full of Devin Thomsens, and not many of them get to have a team and a coach."

He reached back for her hand and pulled it around in front of him. He tried to speak, but gagged on the overwhelming image of when he had found Devin Thomsen down on the East Side.

When Steven got busted, the Coach knew there must be more to it than a bag of pot, and he started to work his own connections of former students and down-and-out friends. Rumors of meth came quickly, and he forged that into an

162

obsession to find Devin Thomsen. Off for the summer, it took Cardsen less than a week to track him down.

A thin woman with hair everywhere and bad teeth and nearly black rings under her eyes let Cardsen in the door. Two gritty men and a woman smiled and laughed at him from old couches like he was the entertainment, but he ignored them. And then Devin, already ghost-like, had come out of the kitchen, hands thrust in his dirty jeans. White hair blending with his T-shirt, just like that time after practice in the coach's office. But instead of looking down, he had his eyes on Cardsen with a stunned expression. Cardsen saw the purple under the kid's eyes, like he was starving to death. He locked Cardsen in an unblinking stare and rocked side to side, too fast, and he forced his face to change to a goofy grin.

"Come with me, you can stay with us."

"I have everything I need right here."

He forced himself to turn and leave the sight. It took every ounce of belief he had in human freedom to walk away.

On the way home he stopped at the Thomsen's apartment to tell Alexa. She answered, but he couldn't bring himself to tell her the details. He gave her the address and suggested she call the police. Alexa gripped his arm with both hands, put her forehead on the front of his shoulder, and cried in heaving sobs.

Cardsen swung his feet up and lay back, turning his head toward Sonia. "Meth. Can you believe it? Steven and Devin. I can't wrap my mind around it. They are just beautiful little kids. And you are wrong on one point, there is only one Devin Thomsen."

His wife stretched her arm across his chest and pulled closer, and Sean continued.

"Do you know what it said in the paper last week? Only eight percent leave behind a meth addiction. Eight percent. I thought, bullshit, nothing can be that low. So I called Christina, you know the one that keeps the teachers sane? She'd know, she counsels everything. So she says numbers are hard to get because of the newness in the level of use, but she said she'd put first time success in recovery for those who try at three to five percent. Most don't try because they're convinced it is not an addiction, or just plain love it. Three percent. What do I do with three percent?"

"Shhhhhh. No numbers, Sean. In the spirit world, it's not done by counting with numbers."

Sean Cardsen worked on breathing, and relaxing every muscle. *What does it teach them if I quit on them? I won't quit on them. Not ever. If I was their platoon sergeant in a war, and there was a three percent chance they were alive, I'd go get them, I know I would. But would I do it for anyone, or just them? Isn't that the real standard? What if it cost me my own life, with a wife and kids at home? Eight percent. Three percent.*

29

The five months after Steven's brief internment for the bag of pot amounted to a furious search for meth and willing girls. He dodged in and out of his mother's house and ignored her desperate inquiries and interventions. Steven had forgotten most of the places he had slept. He was out of school. He hadn't been there since October. Devin lived somewhere else, gone deep into the city with some real hard-core people.

Gary Overman knew how to find Steven, and tagged along sometimes. The kid was fascinated, but still too afraid to participate in a lot of what he witnessed. Somehow, Overman remained committed, in his own manic way, to school and sports.

One weekday, Steven hoped to catch his old house empty as he sought food and maybe a bit of cash. Alan was there, alone, which took Steven by surprise.

"What the hell? I thought they had you living at Christian school."

Alan looked at him. "I got kicked out."

Steven pushed in and moved toward the kitchen.

"Kicked out?"

"I was pissing them off all the time with questions about God."

"They kicked you out for that?"

"Actually, I failed a drug test, THC." Alan stared at Steven, but when he didn't respond, he continued with the story. "Shit I bought from Jensen when I came home for a weekend. I shared joints with a couple of kids in the parking lot. They didn't have any friends, so I became their friend."

Steven noticed Alan staring at him, and he started to twitch. He heard what Alan was saying. He tried to feel something, there seemed to be a message desperate to get in his brain. But Steven found it easy to ignore the attempted intrusion. He felt nothing, and said nothing.

"When we got home this morning, Todd and Mom got in my face, told me I had to go back to rehab camp, where I went last summer. Man, I took her apart, talked all sorts of crap about her, made her cry. Most of it true, some lies. Todd made a move to come at me. You should have seen it, a perfect sweep-single leg like Cardsen used to show." Alan kept his eyes on Steven, but became animated as he demonstrated. "I tripped him straight back. His head bounced like a basketball off the floor."

That was an image that touched something, and Steven laughed, which made Alan smile.

"Todd jumps up, his face as red as that blanket on the couch, and hair sticking straight up. He didn't even look at me, just stormed out to his 4Runner and took off. Mom screamed like it was some kind of movie, and went after him."

"His head bounced like a ball! Alan, why are you staring, dude? It makes me nervous."

Alan finally looked down to the floor. "Because you don't look right. Are you ok? Is it true what Jensen says?"

Steven cut him off. "Why do you talk to that cocksucker? Get your pot somewhere else."

"I miss you here, and I'm leaving."

"Yeah, home sweet home. I'd rather sleep on a floor out at the trailer park."

"Steven, I'm going to Seattle. It can't be any worse than here. Dad's coming down tonight to get me."

Steven spun and shoved a chair across the kitchen floor. Alan took a step back.

"He wasn't enthusiastic about it at all. I'm not sure how things will go. You know, he lives alone, at least that's what he says. So it's got to be better than here. Steven, will you stay and see me off? Maybe you can even come with us."

Tension seemed to fly suddenly from Steven, and he spoke with a calm voice. "No, I'm leaving. You go. Go to Seattle. I've got everything I need down here."

Steven left the kitchen and walked to the stairs. He went up to his room, opened the door, and turned on the light. His mom had been cleaning, moved a lot of things. He stepped inside and looked at the two championship brackets on the wall. He turned back toward the door then paused. He went toward the bed and got on his knees to peer under. Ruff was still there.

30

He looked at a clenched fist, wet with drizzle diluting the deep red color flowing off of it. Steven's fingers pressed in so tight that his forearm might explode. The sting of fresh air meeting the meat exposed from under torn bits of skin reminded him that it was his own fist. He looked away from it and saw the look in Jensen's eyes, a look of curiosity, sadness and wonder. They were frozen there together for a moment, stretched to agonizing length by their stress.

The true length of the pause didn't matter, because it disappeared as he hit Jensen again, the fourth time, looking into his victim's eyes. The strike broke the left cheekbone and tore another piece of skin off one of Steven's knuckles. As Jensen fell, Steven's left fist was already moving, catching Jensen on the right side of the chin and spinning him around, sending him down to the patio on the broken side of his face. A hard kick delivered to a kidney. A sound like air and water rushing came out of Jensen. Leaning over enough to see the now unnatural features, Steven spit on the broken face.

Jensen panted and moved his lips like a fish pulled up on the bank, one eye looking up.

Steven wheeled from the sight and looked at Gary Overman, who took a step back, as if he thought he might be next.

"Dude." Overman, who tried to add a sick giggle, was as close to speechless as he would ever be.

Steven walked past him and went through the sliding glass door. He sat down on a kitchen chair with his head in his hands. Blood and water streaked down from his knuckles and curled in rivulets around his wrists. Outside the rain picked up.

Overman walked in. Steven glanced up at him, eyes dark as coal, and Overman spoke quietly. "Um, I don't know if he's going to get up."

Steven bolted out of the chair and Overman jerked back out of the way. Steven grabbed the phone on the counter. Somehow, he remembered Ryan Van Gorder's number. He'd know what to do.

"Hey, Ryan."

Ryan responded with surprise. "Steven, is that you?"

"Yeah, it is."

"Wow, it's good to hear from you!"

"Yeah, but maybe not. Ryan, I'm at Jensen's and he fell real bad on the back porch, he might be hurt." A thought penetrated to Steven about how robotic and strange his own voice sounded. "But the thing is, I gotta leave right now. I'm not supposed to be here. If you could come over and check on him, I'd never forget that. Ryan, I'd really appreciate it."

"Well, I guess...I mean, it's not that far, but I haven't been over there since sixth grade."

"Ryan, you have to come. And I have to go."

31

"Overman!" Cardsen pulled his feet off his desk where they had resided since the last student left the room. He leapt up and they shook hands two seconds after Overman entered the room. *He came back from high school to visit. One of them came home.*

"Coach! Hey, I miss you coach. How'd you do this year?"

"We took third. The whole thing went by fast. Good kids. But you know, nothing like what we had. Alan never came back." Cardsen embarrassed himself with the sadness in his voice, and went quiet.

Overman turned away, cheeks turning red. "My desk. Right over there. I wrote McCall Sucks under it, but you can't get me now."

"So how is it over there? How's high school?" Smiling, Cardsen settled back into the chair at his desk and put his hands behind his head.

"Oh, Coach, you should see everybody there. People all in black carrying notebooks of drawings, Christian girls with big crosses on their sweatshirts, all these big football guys in letter jackets taking up space. Chicks who look like guys and guys who look like chicks. It's a trip. Man, this teacher I have for Biology, she says 'Hey, you want to teach this class, or shut your mouth?' So I go up and she hands me the chalk and I take off on chemical bonding, just like you taught here. I go for six minutes and she starts crying. This chick told me later that it was because I did it better than the teacher would've.

"And wrestling's going to be sweet. That coach we have over there, he knows everything. I've flat been working out.

Check it, even more ripped than you remember, check this forearm, veins everywhere."

Cardsen had to listen carefully. Overman completed all the information in about twenty seconds. By the time Overman took a breath, Cardsen was laughing. He grabbed Overman's forearm. "Yeah, you're going to be a beast. I always knew it. Can you still do a backflip?"

"I'll turn one now up on your desk in my hiking boots and coat."

Cardsen held out a hand. "No, no, I believe you!"

Overman pulled his arms away and put his hands in his back pockets. Cardsen realized how much the kid had grown in the past year. His braces were off and his face had filled out. He smiled briefly and then his face changed, he looked scared. Overman's eyes searched Cardsen's. "Coach, here's the thing. Did you hear what happened to Jensen?"

"Yeah, I heard. Someone worked him over. Is he going to be all right?"

"He is but for a while he has to have all sorts of wires and stuff for his mouth and jaw. The thing is, I was there."

"At the hospital?"

"At the ass-kicking."

Cardsen pulled his hands down from behind his head and leaned forward, putting one elbow on his desk. Life became serious again. "You're kidding."

"No, and I saw the person do it and it was the scariest thing I ever saw. They arrested that guy today."

"Who?"

"Well, Coach, that's why I came, I mean, I don't know what to say to the cops about what I saw, because it was Steven who did it."

"Steven Matchik?" Cardsen's voice was flat. Overman nodded. Cardsen did not emote, but he was speechless for a few seconds and he didn't realize that his hands were cramping from tight fists that he had made.

When Cardsen could speak again, he didn't have any doubt about what he told Overman. "The truth, Gary. I don't see it any other way. This is the best time for Steven to get in trouble. It only gets worse if you wait. Do your folks know?"

"Nope." Overman shook his head.

"I'll call your dad if you want. He can come here, and I could be with you when you tell him. He may want you to go through a lawyer or something."

32

Cardsen saw the return address on the letter and his heart beat faster as he took it to the kitchen table. He knew where Steven had been sent and wrote him first. Cardsen researched the visitor list. Inmates could only have one visitor a week, prearranged. Cardsen didn't want to undercut the opportunities of Steven's parents by making requests, so he didn't push the issue. He tore open the letter.

Dear Coach,

Thank you for writing to me. I can't begin to tell you how much that means to me. I was so surprised to get the letter.

I woke up today even before they made me get up, which is early. I was kind of disoriented, I mean, how did I get here? Do you think I have always been this way? Is this what you and Coach Waters thought I would be? (Maybe you couldn't tell me because you didn't want to discourage me.)

I'm sure you heard about what happened. Jensen talked about Alan and some things Alan did, and something happened to me and I hurt him. I don't know if you can ever be proud of me again. Tell Gary Overman it's ok that he told the truth, nothing matters as far as that goes. Tell Gary to stay the hell away from everything that he saw with me. He's got a cool family and wrestling and you and his new coach and teachers to guide him. Plus, he already acts like he's on drugs anyway, so what's the point? Sorry, I know that won't be funny to you.

My mom and dad have both been here to visit, separate of course. Kind of hard with my dad, I'd only seen him once since he left. The next time I see him, I'm in here. Rather not get into that, I mean, I only grabbed this one piece of paper. It is good my mom is trying to help Alan, but I don't like her boyfriend, and I want him at Braxton with you and Coach Waters.

I am sober and I feel good. My goal is 100 pushups by the end of the month.

I don't know how to tell you this, but Devin Thomsen, well, he's not like us. He was an interesting friend but I can't help you understand or help him. He and I should have never met, but we had that great season, you know? I am really sorry because you seem to care a lot about him.

The food is ok here, and they are pretty strict, you could say most of my time is isolation. I do not know what all happens here, but I will be here two years, so I guess I will find out. I wish I had gone to wrestling camp with the high school kids, I don't know why I didn't and thanks for trying.

Sincerely, Steven Matchik

33

September, 2005

"Wilson! How about if we go hard today, the last hour we go back and wade in that stream we saw from the bus? Relax under those trees there. Mount Hood will still be here tomorrow for more." Steven looked down the trail at Wilson, who heaved in a full breath of air, expanding his chest against his jacket, which looked as if the buttons might pop off. Wilson had told him he was two-hundred eighty five pounds, and that the NFL should have wanted him, but didn't. The Gore-Tex coat bunched up under his biceps and stretched across his broad back tight as a second skin. "Damn this mountain climbing," he often said, "In Chicago, there would be elevators."

Wilson put his hands to his hips. "Matchik, you gonna be a lawyer someday. Maybe you defend yourself next time, and you don't wind up here."

A couple of the boys snickered without turning their heads and without breaking their strides on the trail.

"You try to make a bargain, and you got nothing to bargain with. So turn around and get back up front."

Steven turned and looked up past the file of boys, to his normal place at the front of the line. He took three steps and stopped again. "Seriously, Wilson, you know we'll work. If we do as much as yesterday in two hours less, and go one more hour after that, you gotta give us an hour by that stream."

"The more you ask, the more you talk, the more I want to keep you working an hour more, not less!"

Wilson tried to look angry, but Steven knew better, so he laughed just a bit and shook his head. Wilson fought a smile, but it came anyway. "Matchik, whatchyou doing here anyway?

175

I know you got family. I bet money, too. Your dad in office, like a politician? You look like that kind, like your people ought to be on TV. I'll bet you had to try to get thrown in jail."

Steven tried to extend his smile by faking it, but that didn't work and he looked down. "I don't know."

During the exchange, Edmonds had closed up his normal distance behind Wilson and peered over Wilson's shoulder. Edmonds was the official guard, essentially the gun carrier. Wilson was the unarmed "counselor," but did most of the "guarding." His enormous bulk gave all the actual physical and psychological advantage he needed.

Edmonds glared at Steven and then cut in. "Wilson, why do you talk to that shit? Look at him, the cock in his walk. He's playing you. That's what we get in this part of the country. Product of liberal panty-waste parents and government. Give them everything, and then they sell their mother for a hit of jib. He's fascinated by you, probably never seen a black man up close. Probably whacks away in his bunk about it."

The guard had come too close though, and he couldn't see Wilson's face and how much he had perturbed the bigger man. Wilson shook his head and blew air through his pursed lips. His head moved a bit but never actually looked back. He kept his eyes on Steven.

Steven spun around without looking up, and put his shovel to his shoulder. Blowing air in imitation of Wilson, he pushed on ahead, shoving his free hand in his pocket. He could still hear the men for a few more steps.

"Why you say that stuff, Edmonds?" Wilson's voice projected up the trail, so Steven knew the man stared up at him, not back at Edmonds.

"Well, you're still pretty new out here, trying to help you understand what you get out here."

"Yeah. So, who is it that's fascinated with who?"

176

Their crew was composed of twelve teenage boys from Steven's assigned "barracks." The prisoners varied greatly in size, three were very large for their age and one obese, but nevertheless they all climbed like mountain goats. Most were small and thin, trying to find some muscle to build after runs on the meth. Two were black, one Hispanic, and three of mixed indeterminate races. Their hair had been reduced to buzz-cuts and they wore light green jumpsuits. Tied around their waists were good quality lined, yellow raincoats. Despite the complaining and the blisters, being selected for "crew" was better than anything back at the barracks. For over a month they worked on the Skyline trail out of Timberline Lodge, where they parked the bus.

Timberline is the destination for the tourists and skiers on the mountain, Mt. Hood. Word had gone around that the lodge was the building featured in the old movie The Shining, so as they entered the parking lot each day, Steven led the guys on their only group act of defiance. They all raised their pointer finger at the same time and moved it up and down croaking "Redrum! Redrum!" louder and louder. In his last letter to Cardsen, Steven told him that it was his favorite part of the day. Steven also wrote how it creeped him out that Jeffers, the guy who always sat behind him on the bus, had killed his own girlfriend yet still participated in their ritual like it was nothing.

Steven could tell that it pissed off Edmonds that Wilson never intervened on that activity, providing another good reason for the ritual. On the subject of contact with people outside their group, Wilson and Edmonds stood together. They arrived at 7:30 each morning and parked in the special spot reserved for them. If an inmate spoke to a hiker or tourist on the job, they were left home the next time out with two days of isolation, lost their spot on the crew, and went on the waiting list to get back on. But the boys couldn't shut their eyes, and most days yielded fleeting views of snow bunnies heading up to the year-around skiing on the glacier. They saw long hair in ponytails, and form-fitting ski outfits, or fatigues for the snowboarders, hinting at earthy muscles underneath. They saw lots of hikers in shorts. Each one catalogued for further discussion and enhancement back at the barracks. That alone made the long, early morning ride and punishing work worth it. The brief visions were the focus of the conversations and bedtime bunk fixations, but in truth, there was more. In his most recent letter to Cardsen, Steven mentioned that the outdoors began to do something to him, something good. He thought about how he would have to expand on that next time he wrote to Coach.

The peak of Mt. Hood, grey and white, always loomed above them as they wound out on the circumambient trails. Walking Skyline Trail, one dips into the scrubby windblown trees that mark the top of the forest, and then back out into the open, moving in a lateral cut at about 6000 feet altitude across the dreary gray basaltic flows. Briefly shrouded but never completely out of view, the faces of Hood supervised them more intensely than the guards. Hood's faces changed with the angles, serene but serious, inscrutable but in charge. A living volcano, it was their Olympus. The gods these boys never knew but had heard others talk about in fervent unintelligible language; the man on the cross, the old guy on a cloud, the pot-bellied Chinese guy, the witches and angels. They all must live up there, inside, behind the glaciers.

For three weeks the crew had been clearing gray till from a landslide covering Skyline Trail just before what some call Zig Zag Canyon. The damaged section lay two miles one way from Timberline. A popular trail for hikers in the summer, word had gotten out that the trail remained cut. So, as the days went by they saw fewer and fewer hikers, though their work had made the route easier to get through.

Edmonds often called the trail a God-forsaken track. He also liked to say that every time you stepped on it you get a punch on your ticket, then one day the mountain will collect on those punches. The crew knew that it irked Edmonds when Wilson would allow Steven to take two or three others and climb over the jumbled mess at the slide, initially a hundred feet wide, and dig back toward them. Only the occasional heads, shoulders, and shovel buckets flinging up high would be visible. Everyone knew they could be miles down the trail before a summons for help would cut them off. Everyone also knew they wouldn't escape. The Forest Service, Sheriff, or Hood itself, which could be one wicked god, would see to that.

Steven had to lead, and it worked out that way over time. He just couldn't stand to walk behind plodders ahead of him. Irritated by Steven breathing down their neck, each crew member asked him forward until he wound up leading the crew. Now, each time they went out, Steven took his place at the front.

When Steven first arrived at the correctional center, the kids from tough neighborhoods saw an easy mark, a suburban ass-wipe who should probably be in a clothing advertisement rather than inside. But when they prodded him into fighting, they found a madman. They brought their hell and experience with serious violence, but he met it with his compact athleticism, innate primalism allowing anything to win, and wrestling moves effective in real fights. Three times he showed his fury, and then served his isolation without comment to either authority or peer. When released, he talked no smack, asked for no revenge or rematch. He didn't avoid his attackers, falling into chow lines near them without comment or evil eyes.

The third time, every kid nearby elbowed their way in to watch. Wilson later confessed to Steven he knew the fight was coming. Steven often rolled Wilson's confession through his mind. He could quote the whole speech to himself. He liked to listen to Wilson's voice in his head.

"You know, Matchik, there was so much chatter I had to see what you were all about, what you had. I figured I'd stop it quick, lobby for two days isolation, and smuggle your books in there. I know how you like your books. You threw Arnold through the air. That I couldn't believe. He's gotta be twenty pounds heavier than you. Arnold is tough, don't misunderstand. He hit you so hard three times I felt bad I didn't move quicker. And you, all sucked down from the queer crank shit you people like, throwing some kid through the air. Sorry about it kid, truly I am. I thought it would keep my job interesting.

Should have just talked to you. That would have been interesting enough."

Steven wasn't sure he forgave Wilson, but the man had apologized to him, and since when did the guards ever apologize?

Four days remained in September, the time coming that Hood would be wrapping itself in its thick, white blanket and shutting down the trails to interlopers. Steven's parents had brought him to Hood in seventh grade, joining the October skiers carving out their narrow intrusion on the monster. Edmonds called it an Indian summer, because already the crew worked later into the fall than others had. At lunch earlier in the week, Steven had overheard Wilson and Edmonds talking about their ranger liaison, Mays, and his concern about the crew. Mays told the guards that he had called his superiors, who said they could only quit when the trail was cleared, as their agreement stated. "Damn them. You don't mess with the mountain!" he said to Wilson and Edmonds. Then the ranger told them he had tried their boss at the Clackamas Youth Correctional Center to see if they'd back out on their end, but the call died at the desk of some secretary. Wilson laughed and said that many calls died there, such as complaints about mail, food contracts, and the bright lights of the facility.

A daily pattern on Hood was clouds for a couple hours, an hour of sun, an hour of alternation, and then clouds again, ending with a thunderstorm about the time they got back to Timberline. Steven knew the pattern, and considered that the day began warmer than most. The sun still shined when they took their lunch. Always one baloney or pb&j sandwich, one fruit, and two granola bars. The boys were lathered with sweat from the work. They hadn't used their jackets, but had brought them along to the level area for lunch and sat on them.

Steven looked up at the peak through most of lunch, not joining in the banter. Two or three others had followed his gaze. The mountain top was disappearing in a swirl of white streaked with silver. They watched the clouds dance and join and stream together, such was their rapidity of movement. Behind the mountain, a wall of impenetrable gray-black clouds soared even higher than the summit, a tsunami looming, but fixed as a backdrop for the moment. The hot air that had blasted them in the morning was shooting up the mountainside and colliding with the cold wall creeping over the mountain.

Wilson looked at Steven and followed his eyes up to the peak. He glanced over at Edmonds, who tore open a king-size Snickers bar.

The radio that Edmonds wore came to life with a loud electrical pop, and the guard nearly gagged on his candy bar. The tone of Ranger Mays' voice could be discerned, but there was too much interference to understand individual words. Edmonds fiddled with the dials and shook the radio. He moved over to Wilson. "Damn it, it's that Mays calling. What do you think he wants?"

Wilson went ahead with a bite of sandwich and talked right through his chewing. "Didn't you grow up in the shadow of this thing? Look up there." He bobbed his head up to the peak and continued speaking. "I don't know mountains, but if I saw that happening at the top of the Sears Tower I'd know what was coming."

"Holy shit." Said Edmonds, awed by what he saw. "Look at that."

Wilson shook his head in disbelief. "Is that the first time you've looked up there in the last hour?"

"Mays wants us off the mountain early, I bet."

"Early? Now sounds good to me. Try the cell phone."

"It never works up here. We can't quit now, what would we do with everyone at Timberline until the bus comes?"

Wilson brought his bulk up slowly and knocked the gray dirt off the rear of his pants. The talk among the prisoners died as they listened to the exchange and they seemed to all rise at once. They moved together so they could hear, and they began to chatter again, with the same collective message. *Stuck in Timberline lodge, with the tourists, the ski bunnies, while it rained outside, maybe for hours. Let's go, let's go!*

Steven didn't gather around the guards, or consider the lodge. He remained where he sat, fixated on the mountain.

That's amazing, beautiful, intense.

God's coming.

God's coming and dad and mom and her boyfriend and my little brother won't even be here to see it.

The temperature plummeted now in whole degrees per minute. The boys scrambled into their lined raincoats.

"Damn, it was hot just before lunch." Jeffers, the one who had killed his girlfriend, had come back over and stood next to where Steven sat.

For once, the nearness of Jeffers didn't creep him out. It didn't matter now. Steven looked up and smiled. "That means it will snow. Button up your jacket."

The wind ramped up in a single wave, from a slight breeze to a cold thirty mile per hour hammering. The temperature plummeted almost instantaneously. In just over twenty minutes, the temperature would drop over forty degrees.

Jeffers leaned over to shout at Steven, annoyed by the self-assured air the kid on the ground had adopted. "That doesn't make any sense. Snow from hot."

Steven pointed up at the mountain crest, disappeared under clouds now nearly black and swallowing the mountain down toward them. He gestured with enthusiasm as he spoke. "The hot air shoots up the side of the mountain. If there is a wall of cold air waiting for it, like there is now, it skips right off and on up very fast into the sky, cooling off so rapidly that the water it carries freezes and collects in ice balls. Then it falls down. The wind is the cold air coming down the mountainside underneath. Snow, hail, sleet, comes from warm air originally, not cold."

Jeffers looked at him like he was about to make fun, then he gazed up the mountain again, which sobered him. "How you know that stuff?"

"School. Science class."

"How come you didn't tell Wilson earlier, get us off this mountain?"

"Because I'm not in charge. I'm not in charge of anything."

Edmonds and Wilson joined the prisoners in a hurried and clumsy effort to get rain hoods out of their collar pouches and tied over their heads. There was going to be no further debate about what to do, everyone knew they had waited too long already. The crew had worked through the misery of rain and wind before, but nothing like this darkness and cold roar. They knew how mucky and slippery the trail home could get.

Wilson moved into the midst of the boys to speak, while Edmonds stepped back and wrapped the remainder of his

Snickers bar for his pocket. "Get your shovels and then fall in behind Matchik. Single file."

At that moment huge cold drops of water began to pelt, mixed in with icy slush. In an instant the wet mixture covered their heads and shoulders. Wilson bellowed but could barely be heard. The wind had reached forty miles per hour and the slush pelted them if they faced into it.

"Fast but steady. No one runs ahead or you're off crew and in solitary. At Timberline you wait outside against a wall until I say otherwise. Now move!"

It took a little over ten seconds to get into formation. They left the site in the same order they arrived, Steven in front and the crew followed by Wilson and then Edmonds. Fingers were already numbing through unlined leather work gloves on the shovel handles.

Two miles to Timberline, just a minor workout of a half an hour in good weather. But on that afternoon, if the next half hour changed as much as the previous one, they might as well be walking through a volcanic eruption of the mountain.

After four hundred yards, it was crisis in full. The wind gusted in unpredictable directions at up to sixty miles per hour. Quick shifts took crew members down before they could adjust their body weight. Ice hammered their faces horizontally, a white coating already on the ground. The trail grew slippery with grey-black, volcanic ash soup and the clumsier members of the crew began to slip and trip every few steps. Others pulled them up and pushed them on. Wilson and Edmonds had closed up tighter behind and Wilson urged them on, yelling to keep going at a strong pace, no running. Few of the crew could hear him, but the message passed up the line.

Up front, Steven had his hooded head forward, pushing like the prow of a ship into the perfect storm. His sure feet bobbed and danced on arch and tiptoe, easily reacting to all his changes in center of gravity. Of all of them, he alone could keep a regular pace, but it would separate him, so he would slow and look back and let the others tighten up.

After getting ahead and letting the crew catch up several times, Steven stopped and stood upright. Perpendicular to the ice, his face felt as if it was coming off. The crewmember behind, head down, bumped into him and looked up at Steven's face, eyes desperate.

"Grab onto my coat tail with one hand. Pass it on."

He grabbed on and then spun to beckon the next boy behind him.

Steven almost threw away his shovel. It only seemed to make sense. People had been nicked by the blades when they slipped. The shovels were slowing down the pace. *Screw the CC's shovels, why risk their lives for a ten dollar shovel for the CC?* He was surprised the crewmembers hadn't already ditched their tools, but they were gone to robotic states. They could only plod on in fear, waiting for instructions they couldn't hear. Despite that, he found he couldn't bring himself to throw away the shovel. Steven wondered if he was the only one still thinking, could that be? What did he know about surviving the mountain?

Soon they would reach a drainage cut, followed by another cut fifty yards after that. The cuts were not quite as big as Zig Zag Canyon, but they would be sheltered a bit as they dipped in, as long as they were not already gushing icy water in a flash flood. Steven turned, dipped his head and pushed on, leading the train. *We might not make it. Maybe we can dig in somehow with the shovels. We may know when we try to leave the second cut. I'm keeping my shovel until then. I hope the rest do, too.*

When they reached the first cut, they gained a brief respite from the wind. Water flowed as a grey soup, but did not yet overflow the small culvert built under the trail. Steven thought he heard an audible collective groan from the crew behind, as if the slightest relaxation brought a deeper understanding of their dire straits. Steven didn't slow much, he pulled them on through and back into the open. He found himself gasping in the shock of the wet cold. His pants were soaked, fingers screaming out in pain on their way to numbness, his face like he was swimming under a frozen lake.

Coats and movement were still protecting their body cores, they were far from a dying state. If blocked by snow, that would change in a matter of minutes. The ice gradually gave way to more traditional wet snow, and visibility went down to about ten feet.

They pushed on to the second cut and through. A three quarter of a mile push out around a bulge in the mountainside lay ahead. They would benefit from having a few more trees above them to cut some of the wind, but the snow was thickening now and soon they would be trudging through it up to their shins. Steven's determination began to fray as he emerged again into the whipping snow. *We throw the shovels, break apart and run for it. Some don't make it but I know I do.*

The kid behind him jerked his coat so hard he nearly fell down. Steven spun around and leaned in face to face. Eyes wide with fear stared back at him.

"Man down back there. They said stop but I don't know, maybe we should run on."

He's thinking the same thing as me. I don't know, maybe we go.

"Wait for me to find out." Steven pushed past him and back down the line, passing each crewmember. He kept expecting to see one collapsed, but they all had hands-on-knees, gasping, eyes lacking hope if they looked up at him. They had all tossed their shovels away. He had counted eight crewmembers when he ran into Wilson coming the other way. The big guard was wild-eyed but had a determined look. He grabbed onto both of Steven's upper arms with his big hands. "It's Edmonds. He's down back here."

Steven followed Wilson back to find Edmonds' form thrashing in the snow and mud just below the downhill side of the trail, howling in an inhuman shriek that had nowhere to go. One of his legs splayed out in an unnatural direction.

Wilson brought his face down close to Steven's. "Leg broken all to Hell, help me get him up on the trail."

Steven nodded and then scrambled down and grabbed the shoulders of the man's coat. Wilson settled in beside him and they dug in their heels to pull. As soon as they began to tug, Edmonds twisted violently and they slipped to their butts in the snow. Edmonds hit at their hands and then tried to grab, wet gloves slipping off their coats. Wilson slid down further on his butt to shout with his face close to that of the injured guard. "Listen peckerwood, we're pulling you up all in one shot, shut it out."

Edmonds' eyes darted all over and he breathed obscenities while pounding his head against the mud. Steven's face appeared and he put one of his leather gloves to Edmonds' mouth.

"Bite on this!" Edmonds' rolled his eyes back and then opened his mouth to let Steven put it in. Wilson and Steven set up again.

"One time, Matchik, all at once! One, two, three!"

They yanked together, but it was mostly Wilson's massive strength that made the difference as they scrambled backward up in the muck to the trail.

The big man and his understudy let the guard plop to his back and they came close together. New decisions would need to be made in seconds.

Wilson opened his mouth to speak, but Steven cut him off. "I'll stay with him. I got my shovel. Go to the front and lead them in. They can hold your coat and you can plow them in."

Wilson shook his head and looked down at Edmonds. "That son of a bitch."

Three seconds went by. They didn't have three seconds to waste. Wilson searched into the kid's dark eyes. Steven smiled. Wilson appeared hopeless for half a second, but then he gave the kid a half nod back. "I'll send people."

With that, Wilson barged by and disappeared into the falling snow with the crewmembers at the tail end of the column turning to follow. Steven thought he could hear him shouting, but then the wind gusted and the sound evaporated. The form of the last boy in line, Steven couldn't tell who, twisted back and looked at him, then the form turned away and the yellow coat disappeared. Steven walked over and looked down at the guard.

The man had spit out his glove and made gurgling noises. He looked up at the boy and swallowed. "They left me. With you."

The speech was all he could manage and his face contorted in pain. Steven reached down and picked up his shovel. He raised it with the point down toward Edmonds' head. The man thrashed and his right hand pawed at the flap covering his pistol holster. Steven saw that and jammed the end of his shovel into the bank on the uphill side of the trail. Then he dropped a knee gently down on the guards left arm, pinning it from thrashing like he was making a snow angel, and put his face close to the injured man's ear.

"I'm going to dig a notch into the bank, get your upper half out of the wind. It's all snow now, no rain. Maybe we get a top over you. I'm going to dig right by your head so we don't have to move you as far."

There was understanding in Edmonds' eyes, along with frustration, and disbelief.

Steven stood up and grabbed his shovel and began to cut into the bank a couple of feet up and to the right of the man's head. With one glove still off, the last feeling in his hands faded. After a summer on crew, the shovel became an extension of him and his motion remained that of a concise and effective machine. Connection to the rest of his body was beginning to fade as well, but the bank gave way before his attack. He tried to be careful, but once he kicked Edmonds in the head, and another time he sprayed the man's face with grey muck, causing him to gag and spit.

Steven stopped digging when he had a cut in the bank into which he could fit Edmonds' shoulders. It wasn't much, just two and a half feet wide and maybe ten inches back in to the mountainside. On his last shovel full, he slipped for the first time and fell hard, just where his eyes could meet the guard's. Over an inch of snow covered the man, but his eyes stared out from under the icicles on his eyebrows, like a deer killed on a winter hunt. Steven saw some of the tiny spikes shake off and fall to the snow below as Edmonds shivered. Steven tried to laugh, but his cheeks were numb and couldn't move right. He hit himself in the face with his hands, but wasn't sure it was happening because he couldn't feel either part of himself.

Then he struggled up to his feet out of the mud, he looked out of his body, separate from it, like a pilot of a sophisticated machine, the way he used to feel before he went out to wrestle. Like at Braxton, when he bounced on the balls of his feet and swung his arms around and knew he was going to win. It was great to have a body. It was great to be in charge of it.

Steven stared down to be sure his hands wrapped the back of the man's collar, pleased that they had done what he signaled them to do. He yanked in an explosive motion, heels driving, and they both shot into the notch, Edmonds' body pinning him against the bank. He struggled out from underneath and went through several contortions to get Edmonds into the notch. Gone beyond pain, the man just stared. Once, he shook his head no, but Steven wasn't sure why.

Lifting the shovel, Steven went to a pile of mud that had come out of the notch. He managed to throw ten shovelfuls of mud onto his guard's legs protruding into the trail. Steven went to one knee. He didn't feel tired, but he knew he didn't have much left. He didn't feel much of anything, but it made him happy to be somewhere beyond where he'd been before. He slid over to Edmonds. He took the man's right hand and fumbled with it until it had the pistol out of its holster. The man looked down to the gun in his gloved hand and back up to the kid's face, and then he did it again. Steven took the man's left hand and put it across his lap, and uncovered the watch face from snow and turned it up so Edmonds could see the time. Steven leaned in to his ear to shout.

"Fire it every twenty minutes." Then Steven smiled. "If it were me, I'd save just one."

He stood up and Edmonds looked confused as the kid stripped off his jacket. Steven stood in short sleeves, and Edmond's eyes narrowed as if trying to make any kind of sense of what he was watching. Then the kid came back down to a knee and put the jacket over Edmonds' head, stretching it like a tent cover over the upper end of the notch in the bank.

Edmonds fought to find strength, and shouted the words. "What are you doing?"

Steven leaned in, this time his expression serious. "I'm going for a run."

Edmonds closed his eyes and shook his head, when he opened them, he was alone.

34

"Are you still going to the bakery?" Sonia touched his shoulder.

Cardsen glanced up at her, and resumed staring out the window into the backyard and the grey morning. He sat at the kitchen table, newspaper open but unread, cup of coffee gone cold. He made a throat-clearing sound but didn't answer.

Sonia spoke again. "It isn't right. I know people do things in their own way, but this..." She choked up and shook with anger.

"It's their right." Cardsen thought of all sorts of obscenities to go with his statement, degrading to gender, sexuality, addicts, families, religions, personalities. He had been spewing vile at various times through the week, angry stabs out of his isolation. This time, he swallowed the rant.

Cardsen feared failing the test God put before him now, much as he had failed the test before this one, the one where he was to guide and teach. He feared that somehow Steven watched him, and could hear the filth he spewed. No doubt Steven loved his parents, despite all the troubles. Cardsen feared the karma of hating those who grieved, and above all, he knew his hate was the same hate Steven's parents might have for him; jealous, inadequate, and ultimately to be regretted.

"What about everybody else?" Sonia had regained her composure.

"They don't know there is an everybody else."

"Do you still want me to go with you? My mom can come take the kids. She's waiting to see if I call."

"You don't have to."

She enfolded herself around his head and shoulders from behind. "I want to."

"Not much of a date."

"No. Not much of a date."

"I'll call Matt. He's coming, too."

Cardsen's fingers wouldn't work right. He couldn't get the key in the lock of the car door. So he waved the keys at Sonia, and she took the duty of driving. On the way, he thought about kids, teaching, coaching, being a parent.

Replaying the past week in his mind tightened Cardsen's gut. The police officer assigned to Braxton Junior High called him out of class to tell him that searchers found the missing boy on Hood —found him too late. The officer didn't even have to say Steven's name. Liselle Wilkins covered Cardsen's class while he went to Matt Waters' room and called him into the hall. He told what he knew to Matt, mixed in with a mass of uncoordinated profanity. Beyond that, there wasn't a lot of emotion until later. He checked out, drove home fine, and called Sonia, who said she could be home in an hour.

Then he drove over to the Matchik's old place and knocked on the door. Todd answered, opening a crack in the door. "Hello Mr. Cardsen."

An awkward silence elapsed as Cardsen realized that he was not going to be invited inside. Words slid away as he tried to capture and assemble them, but in time Cardsen managed to speak.

"Hello, Tony. I wanted to let Steven's mother and Alan and everyone know how devastated I am by what happened and they are in my prayers. I wanted to let everyone know that I am available to help in any way with services or other needs. If Alan is down from Seattle I'd like to see him and offer him my support."

"It's Todd."

"Excuse me?"

"It's Todd, not Tony."

"Oh, right, sorry."

"Coach Cardsen, I don't think it would be helpful for you to come in at this point. Karen's not in good shape, and she associates many things with Steven's time at your school. I'll pass along your offer about services." Todd shook his head with a sad, questioning look. "Very awkward with deciding on a church or someplace else. It's not clear if Steven had chosen to be saved. We'll call you if we need you. Alan is not down from Seattle yet, and I'm sure he'll be occupied when he is here. Thanks for coming. It was kind of you."

When the door shut, Cardsen became light-headed and wasn't sure if he could turn around and walk. *God, if you haven't got room for that kid, then don't bother inviting me either. Look at what these morons did with the gift of their kid.*

Cardsen made his way toward his car. *And me? What have I ever stood for? Doubt, insecurity, lukewarm mumbo jumbo.*

I'd have done worse than them if he were mine.

He spit on their sidewalk and stepped over it as he walked to the car.

At home, he gave himself forty minutes to cry. Afterward, he went to the bathroom and splashed water on his face. He spoke out loud to test if his voice sounded strong before calling Gary Overman, Austin Reichs, and Alfred Rice. He called Katie Gutierrez, but wound up talking only to her mother, asking her if he could bring Ryan Van Gorder over and spend some time with her. In minutes, Cardsen had picked up Ryan and driven to Katie's.

She answered the door with red-rimmed eyes and gave Cardsen a hug. "Oh, Coach, why?"

Cardsen tried to answer, but no words came out. He looked over her shoulder at her parents, shifting awkwardly from foot to foot. Katie released him and took Ryan by the hand to lead him inside. Mr. Gutierrez met Cardsen as he crossed the threshold and they shook hands, Mrs. Gutierrez just behind him.

"Thanks for coming." said Katie's father.

"I needed to." Cardsen nodded his head. "Katie got close to the boys during wrestling season."

Her mother said, "We had no idea how much, until today. Join us in the kitchen. Please, we have pizza on the way."

They ate and talked. Cardsen felt relieved that Katie's parents did not pry deeply into Steven's history. After a time, Katie began to tell funny stories about the boys on the team, and they found their exhausting sadness being pushed away. Mrs. Gutierrez brought out Pictionary and they all played with gusto, Katie sitting close to Ryan.

At home, he talked through the loss again with Sonia and they held each other until late. He wondered if she would ever get tired of having to remind him that he was a good man.

Cardsen rose early and taught a normal day. Christina, his good friend and the district employee counselor, arrived to see him right as the last bell rang.

"How are you, my friend?" Christina sat on a table near his desk.

"Shitty."

"Your tone sounds equal parts anger, and mystified."

"I was thinking sadness."

"That's in there, but that's from the love you have."

Christina sighed, her slight shoulders heaving up and down, and waited. "Who went to his friends and family?"

"I did. Except for one I can't find." Cardsen felt his eyes begin to water.

"That's what I thought. Would you have liked someone else to do that job?"

He stared at her, knowing where she'd take him, but he still needed to hear it. "No. It's *my* job."

She nodded. "Then you are a gift to them, standing firm on the toughest day of their life. Don't you think? You told me one time that your world view is to always be fighting like a soldier, and you know I've encouraged you to moderate that, if you can. But here you are, on the front line. Did you only want the medals that come afterward? Or do you belong right here, right now?"

"I hate this. And I wouldn't rather be anywhere else."

"That's you. That's your gift."

"Shit."

"Yes, I know. Are you angry at the parents?"

"Yes."

"I believe most parents do the best they can with what they have inside. These relationships you build, you can't imagine what is going to ripple out from this."

"That's what I'm afraid of." Cardsen expected Christina to downplay his fear. She didn't.

"Do you trust God?"

"No."

"Did you really believe you could control all of this? All of these people, all of their futures and events? Is that part of your job?"

"I guess not."

She hopped back down to her feet. "Will you make an appointment next week?"

"I'll find the time."

After school, he dropped by his pastor's office, who reminded him that no one holds a patent on what makes a Christian. He assured Cardsen that God was merciful, *blesses the beasts and the children,* and Cardsen would see Steven beyond the door.

Overman came over that night. His mania started to get to Cardsen a bit, but he wound up in the kids' room setting up an elaborate Hot Wheels system, dissipating his energy to them.

The next day, the obituary said the service would be private, family only.

Cardsen and Sonia met Matt Waters at the Oak Street Bakery, which happened to sit catty-corner from the funeral home.

Sonia stamped her feet as they moved away from the counter to find seats. "Agh, this is..."

"You don't need to say it again, Sonia." Cardsen kept his voice gentle.

Sonia grabbed his upper arm. "I'm sorry. He's your boy. I don't need to bring out my agitation about being here." They kissed.

They took their bizarre front row seats on bar stools facing out the plate glass window, coffees and fancy apple pastries in front of them.

Across the street, the hood of a black hearse stuck out of the carport on the far side of the building. Alan arrived with his father. They wore suits and both ran athletically up the stairs to enter the place from the front. Cardsen only saw the back of Alan's head, but he knew all his wrestlers by how they moved. His heart jumped at the sight. He wanted to run across the road, but he only said, "There's Alan." and took another sip of his coffee.

It was a Saturday, so the bakery had strong business. Each time a customer entered the front door, a bell attached to the top made a cheery sound. Once, the bell tinkled and the door remained open, letting in a cool blast of wind.

Cardsen looked over at the door and he registered the oddness of the couple coming in. A large black man in a sort of uniform jacket held the door while a mousy white guy on crutches, hands heavily bandaged, struggled in, guiding a leg set with an enormous fiberglass cast. The injured man settled in loud, banging chairs at a small table at the far corner of the huge picture window. The big man brought over coffee for both, but they didn't say anything to each other. They looked out the window a lot. Kind of like he and Matt and Sonia.

35

February, 2007

For the first time in eleven years, Sean Cardsen didn't coach wrestling at Braxton. During the last couple of seasons, when they ran in the halls or rolled up mats, he'd felt a hundred years old. Allergies and colds turned each season into a marathon battle against snot and drainage. The demanding kids kept coming and so did the attachments, and he loved and hated it simultaneously. Finally, he had turned it over to Matt Waters and voiced big plans to join a rock band that played oldies in the bars twice a month. That season, Cardsen did not attend a match or look in on a single practice.

Cardsen had let football go the year prior, and the extra time with Sonia and his own children seemed a fine thing. He attended many events that he would have otherwise missed.

The band didn't work out. The guys took turns standing each other up, citing scheduling and families so the whole thing faded. At their one gig, a Thursday night at Magellen's in Gladstone, during Neil Young's "Like a Hurricane," a drunken divorcee came to the stage and rubbed herself all over their lead guitarist. When Cardsen got up that Friday to teach, reeking of second hand smoke after getting to bed at two-forty in the morning, he wished it would all go away.

For the first time in a decade, Cardsen skipped the Oregon State High School Wrestling Tournament. If he had gone to the lower divisions at the fairgrounds in Salem, and perhaps looked at the brackets, he could have had the thrill of seeing the name Devin Thomsen, of Medford Center High, and wondered if that could really be the same person. He could have tracked him down, and had that thrilling reunion. He would have seen the blonde demon wrestle with all heart, and make an unexpected run until hobbled by a knee injury in the semi's. Cardsen would have seen all that.

It didn't happen that way. Cardsen spent his afternoons that week watching Braxton Junior High's basketball team play in their league tournament.

Steven had been dead for a year and half when the first email arrived from Devin. The surprise email sent Cardsen's head spinning with a sharp, clear, almost painful joy, like he had inhaled something powerful. He stared at the subject heading; 'Hello Coach Do You Remember?' for a full minute before he could bring himself to open it.

> *Coach Cardsen,*
>
> *This is Devin Thomsen writing, I don't know if you remember me. A while ago I wrestled at Braxton, and I was a messed up little guy. It could be that you don't want to hear from me at all, I hurt others there in a lot of ways. I walked away from the chance to be with caring people.*
>
> *I am sorry to report that I am a drug addict. Then again, I imagine you knew that. Some good news is that I am in recovery and I have been sober for a long time. Sobriety has not been easy for me. Another piece of news is that wrestling continues to play a central role in my life. After several months in a rehab home by Lewiston, I moved to Medford and I wrestled in high school at Center High. I even made it to state at Salem. Did you go, by chance? I hurt my knee and didn't place. I had a terrific coach at Center, he is like family to me. Would you believe that I made the honor roll my senior year? I had a 3.7 GPA. I also won our team's spirit award. I am*

hoping to wrestle and go to college at Southern Oregon.

I would like to make a promise that I'm done with drugs, but I don't make promises anymore. I believe I'm living a new life. Realizing that Jesus Christ is my savior makes all the difference to me. The guys down here call me "The Runner for Christ." I run all the time. Working out is how I am able to settle down enough to sit in class and sleep at night. Sometimes I run twenty miles in a day. I do other things beyond that, but you might not believe them, and I don't want to sound like I'm bragging, because I'm not proud of what I have to do to myself to live this life.

Most nights I go to Narcanon for an hour before I start studying. I go to a church with a large youth group, where I try hard to fit in with the people there. Some of the kids there are afraid of me and I don't blame them.

There are certain people I think of at Braxton. For example, I am forwarding this letter to Coach Waters. Also, I remember a good friend named Steven, who I still wonder about.

I have attached photos of me wrestling at State. Also, one of me with my sisters, who I am trying to help pass school.

Any positive thing that I have done began at Braxton. Someday, I want to be a teacher, and a coach.

Sincerely, Devin Thomsen
PS – I'm sorry.

Cardsen read it in the privacy of his classroom just after school ended that day, and he howled once, open wounds cauterizing. Had he ever been so happy for someone? Who was he so happy for, Devin, or himself? He printed the letter and took it home to Sonia like a proud eight year old who wanted it on the fridge with a magnet.

That night, when Cardsen tried to sleep, he lay down smiling, feeling fifteen pounds lighter, but he didn't sleep. Slowly, his thoughts turned to anger. Time to have the showdown with God. The contest being the usual mismatch.

Years I lay here asking for sleep, wondering if he was alive, or gone like Steven. How many hours of sleep lost? Couldn't bother to give me something, like bumping into his name in wrestling results, or having an intrepid reporter pick up his story. I would have loved to have seen him at State. I would have gone all the way to Medford for a match. Nothing. Missed it all. I couldn't cut it, so You sent him to some better people that could do something. Thanks for that, I prayed for that, so thanks.

And tomorrow, I write the return that tells him about Steven Matchik. Right after I congratulate him on being a miracle.

Thank You for that bitter work. Got any more surprises for me?

Cardsen perseverated for hours, before he faded into a restless sleep. He awoke with a start and looked at the clock, 3:10 AM. Sonia lay sound asleep. She'd learned to sleep through his turmoil long ago. Cardsen did something he rarely did –he shook her awake, and for the first time ever because of a dream.

"Sean, what is it?" She groaned.

Cardsen could see that he'd have to repeat all of this for her again in the morning. "I had this dream."

"Yeah?"

"I met this guy at a bar. He asked me what I did for a living, and I told him I wasn't sure. He asked me if I wanted to go to work for him, or keep doing what I do. I told him I wanted to do what I do, but I wanted the job to be like I remembered it before I found out what could happen in it. This guy looks at me and shakes his head and smiles. He had an ugly face, with scars, missing a couple of teeth. Then he asks me if I had ever seen anything beautiful die and I said I had. He asked me if watching was worth it. I told him that watching was not only worth it, but an honor.

The ugly guy inflated his chest and moved his torso side to side and made a face, like he was making fun of me, accusing me of being haughty. 'Well, well, what have we here? Were you the killer?' Now, that really hurt my feelings and I said 'Of course not!' Then he relaxed and got serious, with concern in his eyes, and said, 'But you know it happened, some don't.'

Then he leaned to me and asked if I had ever seen anything dead get beautiful again. I said I have. Then he asked me, 'Were you the reviver?' I shook my head, I could only look down, embarrassed. The guy answered for me. 'Of course not. But you know that change can and will happen, some don't.' He laughed and clinked my glass and we drank up. Then he got up and threw some coins on the bar. He said, 'Stay a while. Have another.' He walked away."

Sonia rubbed her eyes. "I'm a little confused right now Sean, I don't know if I can sort that out."

"Yeah, I understand, maybe I'll remember it tomorrow."

Devin,

I don't know where to start to express how proud I am of you. So few return from where you were. For years I wondered about your progress and prayed for the things you described for me, just yesterday. Thank you for the pictures you sent. *The wrestling shots show the incredible skills you worked to achieve. Far more important are the skills you have acquired for life. Clean living, dedicated to learning, working for a better future, taking care of self, family and others. I think my heart about bursts with pride and happiness.*

Your faith is an inspiration to me and I know it will lead to a stronger faith of my own. You have been given this gift to go forward. I wish the Savior's blood could get through to me in the way it gets through to you.

Nightly meetings can get tedious, but at times I'm sure they are sustenance. Try to remember, a small price to pay, as the time drags on. You have shown your value for education and proved that you can be a great student! College is not always the paradise that some portray, it has subtle and overt frustrations. Utilize every support offered there. Stay tight with your high school coach and your sponsor. I am certain the type of partying and hi-jinks you witness there will seem like something foreign and silly after where you've gone. Stay open for friends that like the quiet intensity of true athleticism and faith, of sharing and love.

Ryan Van Gorder made it to State, so did Alfred Rice and Gary Overman. They all placed and Ryan lost a close one to take second in the championship. Austin Reichs probably would have gone, but he separated a shoulder the opening round of districts. It's too bad your 3A division didn't wrestle in the same place, or you would have run into them. Hey, also, I had coffee with Eric Lofton the other day. You may remember the little kid who played violin? He is trying out for the lead in the musical for next fall when he is a senior. Katie Gutierrez is the best runner on the track team this spring, she may make state in the 400! Talk about scholarships piling up, she's been a real academic star. If you would like me to pass anything along to anyone, I will do so. Coach Waters got your email yesterday as well, and I anticipate you will hear from him if you haven't already.

How can I tell you this in the same correspondence? Steven Matchik has died. He has been gone over a year. He died while incarcerated, working on a crew on Mount Hood trails. Details have been hard to come by, but the information I like to believe had him helping others to get off the mountain in a storm. He often wrote to me from there, and he became the wide-awake, energetic, charismatic friend we remember, addictions broken by his time there. I believe he died going hard, giving it his all. If you wish to know more details about the time after your lives separated, I can tell you what I know. Choose that only if you want. We can spread it out over years.

Alan is in Seattle and I don't know how he is doing.

Your mother must be intensely proud of you. Tell her hello.

With love for you, and great pride in you,
Coach Cardsen

Throughout the following summer and fall, they kept in touch. The Coach sent encouragements, knowing how first-generation college students can get cold feet. He talked about his kids and inquired about Devin's sisters and mom. Cardsen went light on his leaving coaching, discussing family and time, never implying that exhausting mentorships played a role.

Devin wrote about insane workouts he put himself through, fifteen mile runs in the hills after wrestling four successive opponents to exhaustion. Clean and jerks in the weight room until collapse. He wrote about nightly Narcanon meetings and attached a photo of the large tattoo on his back left shoulder of angel's wings around the initials S.M. and the graphic blood-dripping cross on his right upper arm. He quoted scriptures and twice asked Cardsen to pass along his condolences to Steven's mom. Devin described meetings with the coach at Southern Oregon as he tried to figure out a class schedule that made sense. He wrote about his terrific high school coach and how the man led him by the hand through the financial aid packets.

Tell Katie Gutierrez the truth about me, and
how I stood right beside Steven when we both
went down, and tell her I did nothing to stop him.

After the fall semester at Southern Oregon began, Cardsen had to wait a month before Devin contacted him. Devin conveyed confidence in his school work, claiming that he wrote insightful essays, and that writing emerged as his strength, and *thank God for spell-check.* The college wrestling team had depth at his possible weights and he would redshirt –sit out his freshman year from competition. They gave him a job in the bookstore and Devin enjoyed the experience. A lot of pretty girls stopped and spoke to him, but he couldn't talk to them about the things he knew best, wrestling and drugs.

In correspondence with his former charges, Cardsen projected a face of strength and wisdom, and a message of eternal faith in their success. He hid the contorted face of insecurity, doubt, anger and hero-seeking self indulgence.

From Devin, he received the face of recovery, penitence, and sacrifice. Cardsen suspected another face, contorted by weakness against pounding internal enemies. He was sure of a hidden world where skill gaps began to sink Devin's academics, of indescribable pain beyond the physical, of teeth-grinding desire that could never be met in ordinary ways.

They accepted the views that each wanted to convey, and relished the idea that the positive faces were the only truth they needed to show from their distance.

36

January, 2008

Just back from Christmas break, Cardsen sat at his computer while his class finished a worksheet.

What are the odds he kept going? He hit the search engine and put in "Alan Matchik wrestling Washington." He selected "State Rankings." *If I had done this a year ago I would have found Devin. Why didn't I think of it?*

140 lb. 4. Alan Matchik 18-2 Inglewood H.S.

Cardsen stared at the screen for a full minute, until a student's question broke in and he forced himself away.

By the end of the day, he had seen all of Alan's results for the year and knew the place and date of the Washington State Wrestling Tournament. Cardsen cross-referenced the Southern Oregon schedule and saw that they would be down at Azusa Pacific for their regional tournament. They wouldn't bring redshirt freshmen. That might leave Devin free.

Cardsen sold the idea to Devin. They would go up together, stay out of the way of the family, maybe not even get to talk to Alan, but they'd be there. Cardsen even offered bus fare up to Portland. Devin scoffed at the bus fare, but by the next day, they had planned the trip for mid-February.

***

After accepting the idea of the trip, Devin stared at the wall of his dorm room. Going to Braxton was a risk. Braxton was dangerous. Could Cardsen know that? Seeing the Matchik family, even from a distance, he never planned on doing that. He reached under his hair and ran his finger along the scar on his temple, and began to shake. The time had come to go back there, time to go see his Coaches. *What if I see Katie? Will she speak to me the way she did at that tournament when I was thirteen? Would she slap me? I wonder if she'll marry Ryan after his Mormon mission?*

I know what I'd like to do with her.

He hit himself in the face with both hands. His dorm roommate glanced over and went back to his homework. Devin knew the poor kid was getting used to the freak show, but remained terrified of the tattooed wrestler he lived with.

Can't happen anyway, she's at Stanford. Everyone is gone, it'll just be me. That's a good thing.

37

February, 2008

Cardsen paused at the bottom of the stairs before turning on the light. He stared at the form asleep on the futon on his basement floor. The green light from the LED's on the stereo system reflected in full from Devin's hair and face, which made him appear to emit the same color. In the peace of that morning moment, the kid's face looked thirteen again. The light reflected off his skin but absorbed into the scars on arms and hands. Cardsen noticed the scars the night before, without comment. The Runner breathed audibly, deep in sleep. The Coach studied him a minute longer before he pushed up the switch.

"You up?"

The Runner stretched, pushing his sinewy limbs out in all directions. "Coach, I'm up. I'm up. I never sleep, but I slept here, at least after a while."

"First round starts at nine today, we've got a long way to go."

"Yes sir."

"Can you handle a long day sitting without working out?"

"Yes sir." Devin smiled as he lay on his back. "I'll wear sweats, in case there is a long break."

They left with a kiss and a hug from Sonia, a box of granola bars, and cups of coffee in the holders.

Cardsen wheeled the aging Buick LeSabre out of the drive as Devin spoke. "You have a nice family, Coach."

"Why, thanks, Devin. We're trying, you know?"

"What about Coach Waters, does he have kids now?"

"Naw, they don't seem to be moving too fast that way. None of my business, I guess. But that's why Matt, Coach Waters, can bring along his wife Laurel today. She's turned into quite a wrestling fan since he took over from me."

Ten minutes later, they picked up Matt and Laurel. Matt burst out of the front door of his house and bear hugged Devin, hoisting him in the air. "Welcome home, kid!" He dropped Devin roughly to his feet and began shaking his hand.

Devin beamed. "Thanks, Coach, but I'm not sure I lived here long enough for it to be my home."

"Nonsense. It became your home the day you walked in. This is my wife, Laurel."

As she took his hand, Cardsen noticed how Laurel studied Devin the way one does the finest art.

With four in the car, the conversations in the car stayed light and fun. Devin struggled to participate. Laurel would have none of his reticence. She drew him out in a way that impressed the coaches.

"Tell us about the coast in January. Matt won't take me out there when the sun doesn't shine."

"Thirty foot waves off of Charles' Cape, Mrs. Waters."

"Devin, call me Laurel."

"Sorry. Laurel, sixty mile an hour winds, horizontal rain. It has to be seen, uh, sorry Coach Waters. Well anyway, it sucks you in. Um, I guess literally, if you step outside. But it's like you are under anesthesia, a whole day can go by in front of the window, you don't even know."

Cardsen noticed that Devin became silent and looked embarrassed. Cardsen glanced in the rearview mirror at Laurel. Charmed and smiling.

The drive to the Tacoma Dome was two and a half hours. Part of Cardsen had hoped for some long, deep sessions talking on the way up and back, but he knew that would be too much time alone with Devin, too heavy for both of them. Now that Cardsen had spent four years studying addiction, trying to understand, he didn't need to push Devin for the lurid details. Such a push would be an admission he sought a sick form of entertainment. It was a blessing to have Matt and Laurel along.

At the Tacoma Dome, the group did not intend to distract Alan or his family, so they took seats high up. Inglewood High School had a huge paper sign over their team and fan area, an easy find on the far side of the arena. They quickly figured out which of the three wrestlers in uniforms matching the colors on the sign was Alan. To Cardsen, he still looked like the typical suburban American kid. Medium sized, unremarkable looks, straight brown hair, wide-open eyes moving all over the gym, taking it all in.

He still looks innocent. Cardsen thought. *My God, how looks can deceive.*

Several times Cardsen scanned the fans under the Inglewood sign, no Mr. Matchik, no Mom, no Todd.

"Hey, you guys see any parents?"

"Not over there, I'm sure of it, Sean," said Matt. "If they were here, you think they'd be sitting near the team."

Cardsen looked the other way, toward Devin. The kid's chest heaved and he didn't look good, he dug his fingertips into his stomach. Cardsen prepared to ask him if he was all right, but stopped. He wouldn't force Devin into a lie, which is what he would get. Devin turned and made contact with eyes unblinking and wild in a way that took Cardsen back a few years.

"They need to start the wrestling." Devin spoke in a growl.

Cardsen became sad that even he couldn't take that gaze, it had been too long. So he looked down. "Yeah. They need to get it started."

The tournament had been compressed into two days, with the semifinals and some wrestle-backs being on the same day as the finals, held at night. Cardsen gambled on Alan still being in it on Saturday. Even if a kid ranked fifth in the state, staying alive in the tournament is not a high percentage bet when there is a sixteen man bracket full of quality wrestlers. But this was the day Devin could come, and Cardsen felt it would work out, and here they all were. The semifinals began and the group from Oregon, up in their perch, poured themselves into the action. Six matches wrestled at a time, and they passed the programs back and forth, and picked out those that caught their eye, and drew the attention of the others to the moves.

As the tournament went on, Devin relaxed. He pulled his hands away from his abdomen and let them hang over the armrests, and they stopped shaking. A steady smile settled across Devin's face. He called out moves to Cardsen.

Look at the granby.

Why doesn't he stay with that single?

You can't try to roll through with a cradle that loose.

Sweet fireman's carry, never saw it coming.

How many times can they switch each other?

That guy on mat five, that's courage. I've never seen courage like that.

At the last comment, Cardsen smiled and shook his head in disbelief.

While they enjoyed the action, none lost sight of the other agenda. None of them hid the fact that they scrutinized Alan. Cardsen considered how he might get near Alan. He tracked Alan as he ran up the steps to a portal, and reappeared a couple of minutes later. A bathroom visit. Cardsen mused how intercepting him at the urinal would not be the place for a reunion. Each arm rotation Alan did was studied, along with every bounce on the balls of his feet. As the round moved on, they saw the moment when Alan decided to go down to floor level and begin to warm up in a more serious fashion. Several times, he peeked out of an entry, first in sweats, then in headgear, finally in singlet.

When Alan ran out on the mat, Devin exploded out of his seat and shook all over, only embarrassment in regard to nearby fans trumped the motor inside him, and he struggled back down to his seat.

Cardsen tensed, ready to fly up as well, but instead he blew out a long breath and he settled to the back of his seat.

Alan stalked his side of the mat, a bundle of energy over forty pounds heavier than in seventh grade, ripped and ready. At the whistle, he wasted no time. He went clear to his opponent's ankle and back up to his feet, elevating the leg until the guy went down. Barely four seconds gone. But at State, everyone was capable. The other wrestler, a thick muscled kid from Camas with a mop of curly hair, popped up and escaped in seconds. The action remained non-stop for the first period, rival tigers trapped in the same cage. Each one took turns being flung out of bounds, being reversed after a takedown in dramatic fashion, escaping with feet flying in a blur. At period, with score 6-6, the Camas wrestler chose down position.

High above, Cardsen looked over at Devin, but he didn't return the contact, his gaze riveted to the mat below, his expression rapturous. So Cardsen turned to Matt. "Wow."

"Yeah, wow. Looks like he got some coaching."

"Yeah, not us." Cardsen laughed.

"Yeah, not us." Matt joined the laugh.

On the mat, it became Alan's match. He followed the hips, tight waist and then wrist control, then two-on-one arm bars, continually punishing the man and blocking the efforts on bottom. His opponent became desperate in his frustration and tried a silly roll-through over his own head, and Alan had him cradled for the rest of the period, collecting back points. In the third period, Camas tried to return the favor with a cradle right at the whistle. Alan fended it off and threw his hips across. In the ensuing scramble, he caught his opponent in a pinning combination and ended the match by fall with a minute left.

Five hours of driving, round-trip, and a fifteen dollar admission; each of the men would have given ten times that for the five minutes they just saw. Judging from Laurel Waters' excitement, maybe she would have as well.

"He's going to wrestle for State Champion." Devin said with wide eyes and a flat voice. Cardsen didn't respond, he blew air out through his lips and shook his head. No adjective could be added by anyone who knew wrestling to enhance that statement.

To get a jump on the crowds heading to the nearby restaurants for lunch, they decided to take a break before the heavyweight matches. Cardsen led as they passed by concession stands and bathrooms on their way to a main exit. Matt hustled up to walk beside him. "Well, are we going to go see him?"

Cardsen stopped and pulled his raincoat on. "He looked so good. We can't risk throwing him. No way. I couldn't carry that on my conscience."

Outside, Cardsen pointed up a street and described a bar and grill a half a mile away. Devin stopped as they neared the crosswalk.

"Coach, I'll meet you there, I'm going to run some laps around all the parking lots here. After that, I'll head over there."

Cardsen looked at him and laughed. Then something inside him jumped. A tinge of worry at any separation. Cardsen glanced down toward the old Tacoma Waterfront. Cleaning up now, but for years the area had been a Mecca for tweakers. Pierce County Washington, the Methamphetamine Capital. With a little too much authority, he responded. "You better be there, because we are going to have one beer, and then I'm going to order a burger for you."

Devin smiled, as if to disarm. "I'll see you there, Coach."

38

The rain had stopped but the pavement remained wet, and little splashes went up from his shoes with every stride. Devin circled the large parking lot to the other side of the dome. Looking in toward the arena, he saw a service entrance with its garage-style door open. Jogging on for a moment, he stopped, did a double take on the entrance, and then ran toward it. His Southern Oregon gear looked like a high school uniform. Devin ran right by the security guard, who sat on a folding chair holding an ancient transistor radio, engrossed in the cackle of a basketball game.

The hall from the entrance led past the humming physical plants that powered the stadium and led directly to a portal that opened out on to the floor. He could see that three heavyweight matches were still going on. Looking up in the stands, Devin located Inglewood and saw no sign of Alan. His experience at the Oregon tournament the previous year made it easy to figure out how things worked. There would be meeting rooms converted into warm-up areas and home bases for officials. Devin looked across the stadium floor to the portal they had seen Alan come out of earlier in the morning. He turned back to the hall that appeared to encircle the floor and ran around in that direction.

Devin scanned three meeting rooms and jogged down a couple of arterial hallways. Wrestlers, coaches and officials of all possible descriptions and uniform colors moved in all directions; laughing, crying, yelling about matches, demonstrating small moves, heads buried in hands, bare torsos with singlets down, heavy sweats with hoods up. Empty food wrappers and plastic energy drink bottles formed a layer on the floor. Devin knew to move away from the crowds, far down the halls to lonely domains.

Alan sat on an empty roll cart for metal folding chairs. His sweat bottoms were on, but his top off and he still wore his singlet. A large plastic water bottle sat between his legs. His hair was tousled and he had a nasty looking bruise on his face. The bruise seemed to ride directly on the cheekbone, showing him to be sucked down from weight loss. Alan's back pressed against the wall and his knees bent up so he could fit on the cart. He had a book in his hands, *All The Pretty Horses*, and he didn't look up when Devin came near.

"Reading for an assignment?"

Alan glanced up but didn't make eye contact with his inquisitor. "Yeah, but it's all right. I like it, except it seems to be half in Spanish."

"I read that last year, I liked it. You wrestled a great match, Alan."

At the sound of his name, Alan met Devin's eyes, face quizzical. Devin thought he saw a flash of recognition, then Alan shook his head as if to chase a thought away.

"I'm Devin Thomsen. We were together at Braxton."

Alan's back snapped up straight, and his eyes widened. He took on the expression of an animal unexpectedly trapped. The book rolled out of his hands and his arms crossed his chest to grab opposite triceps, as if he became cold. But he looked right at Devin. "What are you doing here?"

"I came up from Braxton with Coach Cardsen and Coach Waters."

Alan took on a confused look and tried to speak, but nothing came out.

"I've been sober twenty months. I wrestle at Southern Oregon, but I'm not varsity." Devin stared without blinking, and Alan shivered.

"I don't know what I should say about Steven. I only found out last spring when I got in touch with Cardsen. Your brother should be here, not me. I didn't help him at all, I'm sorry." Devin took a step back, sensing that Alan felt boxed in. He closed his eyes tight for couple of seconds and then opened them, the roar began to build inside of him, but he continued to speak. "You are an awesome wrestler, your breakdowns and rides are amazing."

Alan scooted to the edge of the cart and put his feet to the floor, and found a way to respond. "How did you get sober?"

"I'm not quite sure, God put me with some people, I guess."

"Yeah, well, God didn't see fit to put my brother with those people. Are the coaches coming down here?" Alan nodded down the hall.

"Cardsen is afraid it will throw you."

Alan gave a sardonic smile. "Nothing can throw me anymore."

"That's what I figured."

"Seeing you threw me for a minute, but that doesn't matter for wrestling. If I'm good enough, I'll win tonight. If the other guy is better, he'll win."

"Are your parents here?"

Alan put his chin on his fists and his elbows on his knees. "Naw. Got in a big brawl with my mom on the phone. I've got a girlfriend, and I spend a lot of time with her family. My mom is mad that I am going to hang out with them here. So I told her I didn't want her to come, but now I wish I hadn't done that. My dad had to work. His boss told him he had to work on his case all weekend. My dad says this lawsuit they're doing could pay his retirement and my college."

"Maybe you could hang out with us for a while after your match tonight."

Alan shuddered for a moment and turned his face down the hall. "I doubt it. I'm going to go with my girlfriend's family right after. They have a late-night restaurant picked out and all. You know, I only knew those coaches one year, and I never even had them as teachers. I can't believe you came all the way up here for this. Something happened to me through everything, and I hardly remember anything about seventh grade, I don't even know if I'd recognize them. I'm embarrassed about that. I remember it as a great year. It's when I started wrestling, and somehow it's never ended. One short season together, I don't know."

Devin reached up and rubbed his temple scar as he spoke. "I think...I think that Cardsen's years are longer somehow. He acts like that year is still going on."

Alan looked up again and nodded. "You must be right about Cardsen. I did see the names of those Braxton guys that did well last year at state. I saw it on the internet. I didn't think to look for you."

"I wouldn't have either."

Alan stood up and turned around and grabbed his book, water bottle and sweat top. He spun back and walked past Devin. Then he stopped and looked Devin in the eye from less than two feet away. "Was my brother insane?"

"Your brother was my friend. Your brother was your brother. He wasn't insane."

Alan nodded. "Thanks for coming. If I don't see them, tell Cardsen and Waters that. Tell them I could say a quick 'hi' before I leave, if they can catch me. Come with them so I'll know who they are."

"You'll know them. Everything is still in your mind, but you've had to keep it down, like I do."

Alan raised his eyebrows.

Devin spoke once more. "You know, we made it up here in two and a half hours. You could call your mom, there's plenty of time before the finals."

Alan broke contact and walked away, answering without looking back. "I think I will."

39

"Look at her, the one that walked by the window. She's a tweaker for sure." Cardsen turned from the window and fidgeted, crossing his arms to try and calm himself.

"Sean, you need to relax. Devin is coming. That boy will be here any moment, I can promise you."

Cardsen knew Laurel was sincere, but he found the comment condescending. *You don't know him.* Cardsen didn't speak what he thought. "Yeah, you're right. Any minute now."

Matt began a conversation about the Olympic Peninsula, and Cardsen poured himself in.

Ten minutes flew by and Devin came through the door. Cardsen jumped up from his chair. As he did so, Cardsen thought he saw Matt look at Laurel and shake his head.

The lunch refreshed them. Cardsen never asked Devin about his run around the dome. The group shared some laughs and then made their way back to the arena, where they enjoyed a long afternoon of great wrestling in the consolations.

The finals that night were full of intensity and spectacle. A packed house of over fifteen thousand, the fans primarily knowledgeable wrestling veterans, supplemented by pockets of ignorant high school students supporting their friends, and some terrified mothers.

Tired fans revived, upsets appeared, wild moves were thrown, gesticulating referees drove home their controversial calls.

Winners leapt in the air and hugged coaches. Losers meandered off the floor with slumped shoulders and tears, carrying warm-ups that dragged the floor. They came as close as one can be to a dream and still fall short.

Time and again, Cardsen watched Alan on the other side of the arena and thought about Steven. He noticed that Alan must have a girlfriend. She spoke to Alan a few times, and their subtle interactions indicated closeness. But for the most part, Alan kept a physical distance from her. He appeared to be polite and courteous to the teammates there to support him, but did not give the impression he had intimate friends. His coaches seemed competent and solid, not out to present their own macho case.

All this Cardsen could see and read from far away.

When the time for the match came, Cardsen realized he wasn't at all on edge. He wondered at all his effort to get there, all the anticipation. He fantasized of a Hollywood ending–local boy overcomes tragedy and makes good in triumph of human spirit with proud elders looking on. Like anyone with a pulse would, Cardsen dreamed of that. Yet he realized looking down to the arena floor that no end point loomed tonight, just another step.

A win, and someone would do a feature on Alan's story, impressing some people. Then he would have to decide if he should make his life about sharing through this sport, teaching others about reaching goals through sacrifice, the traditional redemption through sport.

A loss and Alan retained his anonymity. The philosophical master of pain, filled with quiet wisdom to be unveiled at a few unexpected times to change the lives of others.

Cardsen turned to Devin and patted his forearm to get his attention. "Hey, what happens doesn't matter, does it?"

The Runner for Christ looked back, eyes burning with intensity. "No sir. It only matters if he goes hard."

"He will."

"Yeah, he will."

And Alan did go hard. He brought a ferocious determination to initiate and complete moves. His opponent had pure strength, top of the line. Nevertheless Alan found his way underneath and completed a fireman's carry, just like Steven used to do to him on the living room floor. He controlled the hips, he worked patiently toward a cradle, but his opponent was too good for that so Alan put a leg in and started trying to work turks. The other wrestler stayed confident in the face of Alan's onslaught. He kept away from his back and waited for Alan to overdo it and create some looseness and space in the leg ride. That led to a reversal and a tie score.

The match stayed that way, not much flying around, just intense battles down on the mat for control. Switches, arm bars, blocked sit-outs, leg rides, turks for back points gained and then the move lost. When it ended, both wrestlers got up slow, muscles in spasms.

40

Cardsen and Waters placed themselves where Alan would most likely come by on his way back up to the Inglewood seating area. Devin wouldn't accompany them. He said that Alan seeing him wasn't needed. Cardsen didn't put up a fight. Devin and Alan coming face to face would be a complex meeting any way one cut it.

Alan came up the stairway. His coaches knew he'd never take the elevator. He wore his sweats and carried his headgear, a nostril plugged to stop a bleed. As soon as he cleared the top stair he saw them. He walked over without a word and wrapped his arms around Cardsen, put his head against the man's chest, and stayed there for several seconds. He let go and did the same to Matt Waters.

Afterward he looked over to Cardsen and smiled a bit sheepishly and looked down as he spoke. "Sorry. Second again, I guess."

"No one standing here cares. You were amazing, something we'll always remember."

"I'll be in Braxton next month. Maybe I could stop by. My mom is moving away from there, so maybe I should. I may not get back there anymore."

At that moment, two Inglewood students spotted them and rushed up interrupting and congratulating Alan on his work. He looked past the students to his old coaches.

"Thank you. I'll see you."

"Yeah, we'll see you." Cardsen said.

"Enjoy your evening, Alan. We're so proud." said Waters, clearing his throat, and fighting to keep his face composed.

On the way back to their seats, Cardsen grabbed Matt's upper arm to stop him on the busy concourse.

"Matt, could I come back to coaching wrestling next year, as your assistant?"

"Are you kidding?" Said Matt. "What do you think?"

41

Cardsen talked most of the way to Union Station, contrary to when Devin had arrived. As they skirted across the northern part of the city, concrete walls on the freeway blocked any glimpses of the routes to the southeast side, the gritty blocks where Devin had disappeared into that other world over four years prior. Cardsen threw out encouragement and belief statements about the future. They reviewed Alan's matches again and Cardsen's expression carried only smiles. Devin laughed a couple of times and they talked about how at least monthly emails from college had to follow.

They crossed over the river downtown and Cardsen leaned over both hands on the steering wheel of the truck to look up at the construction cranes. "Look at that Devin, another set of yuppie lofts. Took out another block of the old stuff. Man, it was *tough* down here, but so much character. No more Jack London Hotel, no more Chinatown, no more of *that*." Cardsen sounded almost sad.

Devin just nodded and smirked, thinking.

I smoked up at the Jack London. Some dirtbags tried to grab me there. I ran to Waterfront and slept freezing under the Hawthorne Bridge. But it felt great anyway. I can never deny that.

Don't need it now. History. Wait 'til I make varsity at Southern and Cardsen comes to watch, he'll come all the way down there.

The entity inside of him began to move, but he chased it away with a thought of the affirmations, and the blood of the Lord. He missed Cardsen's last ramble, so he just looked over at him and faked it by nodding and smiling.

At the station, they gripped in a fierce, quick hug, and that was that. Neither one could afford to treat the parting as if it would be a long time until they saw each other again.

A straight shot really, the bus goes right down I-5, maybe seven hours to Medford. A few stops in the towns on the interstate, and the small detour to hit Albany and Corvallis.

In the bathroom in Corvallis, Devin looked up into the mirror while he washed his hands. He couldn't hold his own stare and looked down again to his hands as he pulled them from the water and reached for a paper towel. He scratched at a burn scar on the back of his right hand and it only itched more. His insides turned a bit and he prepared for a howl from inside but it didn't come.

He could pay his mom back. His little job in the bookstore at Southern Oregon could take care of that in a few weeks. The lady at the counter said in an hour there was a run out to Newport on the coast, so he pulled his mom's credit card out and bought the ticket. The agent said the smaller bus lines interconnected all the way up the coast to Astoria, right through Lewiston and all the others.

The rain drummed steady on the roof and windows of the bus, but he could still tell that the drive west to the coast was beautiful. He wished he could see the trees more clearly. He thought about Les up at the home in Lewiston. It would be great to surprise him, to show him. Devin smiled, but it didn't last, he just couldn't hold onto the image.

The Runner for Christ leaned his head back and blew all of his air out, digging the heels of his hands into his forehead.

This is stupid, my God. Lewiston is nearly straight west of Portland, backtrack all that way, and slow on 101. Every minute I'm farther from what I am supposed to be doing.

You know why you're going.

To see Les and the guys, to show them it can be done. Show them who I am now, what I look like. And see Dr. Washburn. She's kind of hot, and she taught me the affirmations.

I have chosen to leave the life of drugs...

Shit. Really? You're going all the way up to Lewiston?

Serving others... I'll ask Les what I can do down south for guys like me.

Guys like me do things like this because they know the bus will pass by Nehats, and Arthur's friends are probably still there and I know how to score there.

And it will be like nothing ever before. It will be better, that first hit, I can't wait, it's been so long, and I will be who I am supposed to be, who I really am.

Jesus, say something to me Lord. Your blood. My blood.

Devin pulled his knees up and buried his head down. The few others on the bus remained oblivious to the war in their midst. They read or chatted or stared at the window, and thought nothing of the college boy sitting near the back.

"Kid, you gotta get off."

Devin looked up at the driver who leaned against the seat in front of him, a haggard looking man in a uniform shirt with three open buttons and a dirty white t-shirt underneath. The man sucked on a toothpick and tapped on the luggage rack above.

"I was sleeping, I guess." Devin's body moved herky-jerky and he struggled to stand, bumping his head on the rack above.

"Yeah. Well. It's Newport. You all right?"

He wriggled out to the aisle and slid past the driver. "I'm all right." Halfway down the aisle he turned back to the driver. "Do you go back to Corvallis?"

"In ten minutes I swing it around."

Devin paused and stared at him without blinking, his arms moving all over, as if he had some sort of palsy.

"Are you all right?"

"I'm all right. Where are the offices for those coastal bus lines?"

"Across the street."

Devin could smell the ocean air. The rain had stopped, and the sun hid as a hazy ball in the clouds, preparing to set. He tried to hear the waves but he couldn't. He wanted to run the beach at Lewiston. He wanted to taste sea salt.

He wanted to taste salt in his mouth, dehydrated after a night of smoking shit out of Arthur's shed.

He wanted Steven to be there, both places.

For twenty minutes he squirmed on the wooden bench outside the little ticket office, which doubled as a kite shop. Three times he fingered the worn paper out of his wallet with the phone number of his sponsor in Medford.

Relapse does not have to happen. I have God-given athletic ability.

Relapse is statistically likely.

"Young man, are you going to buy a ticket in here?" A middle aged woman stood holding open a screen door. He stood and followed her inside. A map mounted on the wall behind her displayed color-coded lines. He tried to focus.

"There's a line south?"

"Yeah, the Sand Skimmer, runs to Florence. There is one more tonight."

"You can go inland, maybe to the highway, the 5, from there?"

She turned and pushed her glasses up to look at the map behind her, mounted above a table with a hot plate that held a tiny teapot. "To Eugene, but it won't leave from there until the morning."

"Does it stop near the Greyhound so I can go south to Medford?"

"It stops right there where the Greyhound loads."

Devin nodded. "And north? Toward Lewiston?"

The woman turned back to look at him. She looked down after just a moment.

"That's totally opposite."

He didn't respond. He stared at her without blinking, and she began to fidget and then knocked an open magazine off of the counter when the teapot suddenly began to whistle. She turned quickly and picked the teapot up and glanced at a stack of cups and then over her shoulder at him. She seemed to think better of it and set the teapot down on a hot pad. Devin saw her glance at the phone mounted on the wall next to a poster with neatly stenciled emergency numbers.

"Well, it's lots of stops, every little place you'd ever want on the coast, but you'll make it. It's Cloud Lines north, parked right over there by the Sand Skimmer that goes south I told you about." The woman returned to the counter, took a deep breath, and looked him in the eye. "You don't know where you are going?"

Devin was already pulling out his wallet.

He bought the ticket, and walked outside.

He walked toward the buses parked there.

Parked side by side.

The Author

Jeff Bibbey has been a teacher, coach and mentor for well over twenty years. He resides with his family in Northern Colorado.

CPSIA information can be obtained at www.ICGtesting.com
Printed in the USA
LVOW041003100911

245705LV00002B/1/P